LONG LOST

LONG LOST

JACQUELINE WEST

Greenwillow Books
An Imprint of HarperCollins*Publishers*

Long Lost
Copyright © 2021 by Jacqueline West
Interior art copyright © 2021 by Anna and Elena Balbusso

All rights reserved. No part of this book may be used or reproduced in any manner whatsoever without written permission except in the case of brief quotations embodied in critical articles and reviews. Printed in the United States of America. For information address HarperCollins Children's Books, a division of HarperCollins Publishers, 195 Broadway, New York, NY 10007.
www.harpercollinschildrens.com

The text of this book is set in 12-point Cochin and McKennaHandletterNF.
Book design by Paul Zakris

Library of Congress Cataloging-in-Publication Data

Names: West, Jacqueline, author.
Title: Long lost / by Jacqueline West.
Description: First edition. | New York, NY : Greenwillow Books, an imprint of HarperCollins Publishers, [2021] | Audience: Ages 8-12. | Audience: Grades 4-6. | Summary: Feeling lonely and out of place after her family moves to a new town, eleven-year-old Fiona Crane ventures to the local library, where she finds a gripping mystery novel about a small town, family secrets, and a tragic disappearance.
Identifiers: LCCN 2021005694 |
ISBN 9780062691750 (hardback) | ISBN 9780062691774 (ebook)
Subjects: CYAC: Sisters—Fiction. | Books and reading—Fiction. | Guilt—Fiction. | Supernatural—Fiction.
Classification: LCC PZ7.W51776 Lo 2021 |
DDC [Fic]—dc23
LC record available at https://lccn.loc.gov/2021005694

21 22 23 24 25 PC/LSCH 10 9 8 7 6 5 4 3 2 1

Greenwillow Books

To the librarians

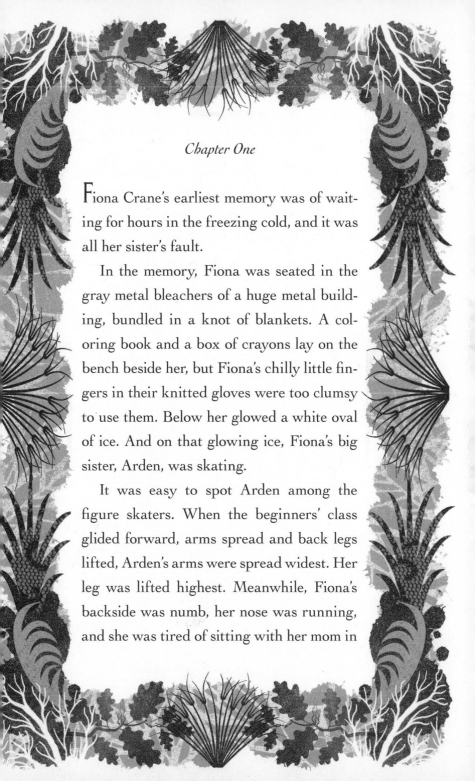

Chapter One

Fiona Crane's earliest memory was of waiting for hours in the freezing cold, and it was all her sister's fault.

In the memory, Fiona was seated in the gray metal bleachers of a huge metal building, bundled in a knot of blankets. A coloring book and a box of crayons lay on the bench beside her, but Fiona's chilly little fingers in their knitted gloves were too clumsy to use them. Below her glowed a white oval of ice. And on that glowing ice, Fiona's big sister, Arden, was skating.

It was easy to spot Arden among the figure skaters. When the beginners' class glided forward, arms spread and back legs lifted, Arden's arms were spread widest. Her leg was lifted highest. Meanwhile, Fiona's backside was numb, her nose was running, and she was tired of sitting with her mom in this skating rink, waiting for her big sister to be done.

But as Fiona was already figuring out, even at three years old, that was life with Arden Crane. Watching. Waiting. Squeezing your life into whatever space was left for you.

Now eleven-year-old Fiona Crane was learning that life as Arden's sister could mean something even worse. It could mean packing up your possessions, moving across the state of Massachusetts, and ending up in a little town named Lost Lake, miles and miles from anyone you know.

With a deep breath, Fiona hoisted another box out of the stuffy moving truck.

The house the Cranes had bought was called a colonial—not just because it had a long, flat front with shuttered windows, but because it had been built in colonial times. It had floorboards that groaned, and windows with tiny panes, and doors that had shrunk or swollen until they didn't quite fit in their frames. "That's just what happens with old wood and changing temperatures," her parents said about the doors that creaked open on their own, or that refused to stay shut in the first place. Fiona's parents always knew the rational, scientific explanation for strange things.

Fiona liked rational, scientific explanations. She also liked strange old things—the older and stranger the better. Someday, Fiona would become either a historian or an archeologist, whichever turned out to be more interesting.

It wasn't the age of the house that bothered her. It was how different it felt from the house back in Pittsfield, the house that felt like *home*. Plus, there was something weirdly dense and heavy about the air in this place—not just in the house, but throughout the whole town. Like maybe Lost Lake was so full of its own memories that there wasn't room for Fiona's family in it at all.

Fiona hefted the box up the creaking stairs to her new bedroom.

The door had closed itself. Fiona kicked it open. Stepping inside, she plunked her box down on a stack of other boxes, then spun back toward the door. Which was closing itself.

Again.

Fiona was trudging back down the staircase when a blur of black and purple flew past.

"Mom?" Arden called, dodging around Fiona so lightly that the steps didn't even squeak.

"In the kitchen!" their mom called back.

Arden flitted toward the voice. Fiona tagged after her, like a slower, shorter shadow.

Fiona and Arden looked very much alike, as long as you didn't look too closely. They both had their dad's brown eyes, long eyelashes, and dark hair, although Arden's hair always stayed sleek and Fiona's was prone to tangles and frizz. Arden had inherited their mom's pointed chin, while Fiona had gotten her dad's square jaw, which made her look even more stubborn than she was. Arden was also five inches taller and moved like a dancing hummingbird, while Fiona moved like something cautious and short legged. Something like a guinea pig.

"Mom," said Arden, darting into the kitchen doorway. "What are you doing?"

Their mom looked up from a pile of boxes. A smudge of newsprint streaked her forehead. Her right hand held two coffee mugs, and her left clutched a wad of newspaper. "You're kidding, right?"

Arden shook her head. The tip of her ponytail whipped Fiona's cheek. "It's three thirty!"

"What?" Their mom glanced at the oven clock, which wasn't programmed yet. She set down the mugs and pushed her springy red hair back from her forehead, leaving another smudge. "Already?"

"Mom, please," said Arden. "I can't be late!"

"Okay." Their mom sighed. "Get your bag. I'll meet you in the car."

Fiona watched her sister flit out of sight. "Arden has to go to practice, even on moving day?"

"Not great timing, I know." Her mom rinsed her

4

hands in the sink, groped at the refrigerator handle for a towel that wasn't there, and wiped her palms on her jeans instead. "You'll have to help your dad finish unloading, ladybug. If we don't return the moving van by five, we get charged for another full day." She planted a kiss on Fiona's forehead as she passed. "Thanks for being a team player."

Moments later, the sound of the car roared through the house and dwindled away.

"Well, Fifi!" called her dad from the front door. "Ready to play beat the clock?"

The day was hot for mid-June. Inside the moving van, the air was stifling. Fiona clunked up and down the unloading ramp, her face prickling with sweat, her muscles growing rubbery. The heat seemed to needle its way beneath her skin.

It wasn't fair that she and her dad were working alone. Not when the entire reason they'd moved to this town was for Arden, so that she could be closer to her figure skating club in the Boston suburbs. Her mom and dad kept saying the move was for the whole family, that it saved one of them from having to make the four-hour round trip with Arden four days a week, that it gave them all more time.

But they wouldn't have lost the time in the first place if it weren't for Arden.

"Quarter to five!" cheered Fiona's dad as they carried in the last load. "Exactly enough time to get to the rental place." He lifted his hand for a high five. Fiona slapped it with her sweaty palm. "All aboard, Fifi!"

"Hey, Dad?" Fiona shouted before he could jog away. "If we're dropping off the truck, how are we going to get back home?"

Twenty-five minutes later, they were pedaling their bikes out of the truck rental lot into the unfamiliar streets of Lost Lake.

Fiona followed her dad past an ancient brick post office, a town hall with stiff white columns, and two churches with steeples sharp as nails. Monstrous oaks and maples layered the streets with shade. Even though it was only five thirty, most of the downtown businesses were already darkened for the night, their signs flipped from OPEN to CLOSED. A thick hush dampened the air.

"Hey!" shouted her dad as they pedaled down Main Street. "An ice cream parlor! We'll have to try it sometime!"

Ice cream? Fiona looked up, surprised. Three-fourths of the Crane family—the three-fourths that were an anatomy professor, a nurse practitioner, and a future Olympian—were intensely healthy eaters. If her dad was offering ice cream, he must be trying to cheer up the one-fourth of the family that was going to be an archeologist-historian and eat whatever it wanted.

Fiona followed her dad's pointing arm. Like everyplace else in downtown Lost Lake, the ice cream shop was closed. The wire chairs and tables on its sidewalk looked stiff and unwelcoming, more like barricades than furniture. The blue awning above the door flapped listlessly.

Something about that empty shop mixed with the emptiness inside of Fiona—the emptiness where her old house and friends and life belonged—making it darker and deeper than before.

"Hey, Dad?" she called. "Do you think we might ever move back to Pittsfield?"

Her dad glanced over his shoulder. "Move *back*?"

"Like in a few years, when Arden can drive herself to skating practice, do you think we'll move again?"

Her dad checked a street sign before signaling a left turn. "I guess it's *possible*. But it's not very likely."

An invisible rope began to wind around Fiona's ribs. "Why not?"

"Well, your mom's job is pretty mobile. Wherever there are kids, they need pediatric NPs. College teaching positions are rarer. If I'd been offered another position in the Boston area, we might have moved east years ago."

The pressure on Fiona's ribs pushed harder. *Years?*

She could almost see her life erasing itself around her, the path that led backward disappearing, and any path that might lead forward devoured by the shade of Lost Lake's giant trees.

By the time they'd pedaled back to the house on Lane's End Road, Fiona felt not just empty, but sweaty and smelly. She dragged herself upstairs to the shower. It wasn't until she'd climbed into the spray that she remembered her shampoo and conditioner were still buried in boxes somewhere. And it wasn't until she'd climbed out again that she realized the bath towels were still packed up too.

When she finally slumped, dressed and dried, back down to the kitchen, her dad and two boxes of delivery pizza had beaten her there. Ice cream *and* pizza? Her dad was pulling out all the cheer-up-Fiona stops.

"Daniel's House of Pizza." she read the box aloud. "Why didn't you get Pizza Hut? Or Papa Gino's?"

"They don't have those here." Her dad flipped the box open. "But I'm sure this is great."

It wasn't.

The pizza was cut into little squares instead of wedges, which was bad enough, as far as Fiona was concerned. On top of that, the sauce was bland, and the crust drooped like a piece of wet fabric.

"Hmm," said her dad, after a minute of quiet chewing.

"Well, new things always take some getting used to."

The sky beyond the windows was just starting to smudge with darkness when Fiona gave up on her last square of pizza and headed upstairs to her room. She kicked open the door, flopped down on the bed, and pulled her hand-me-down laptop from her backpack.

And, like he knew she needed it, an email from Cy was waiting.

Hey! How's Lost Lake?

One more week until my birthday party! My mom already got our tickets, so we can see the Wonders of Egypt exhibit before we visit the rest of the science center. You should wear your cartouche shirt. Nick and Bina and I are going to wear ours too.

Have to get to soccer. Check the attachment!

Cy

The attachment was a photo of a hieroglyphic message. Last fall, Fiona and her friends had taught themselves the alphabet in Egyptian hieroglyphs. They printed T-shirts with their translated names and passed notes during class that no one else could read. Fiona scanned the row of symbols. Quail chick, reeds, owl . . .

We miss you.

Fiona's heart rose and ached at the same time.

It had taken her ages to make real friends. She had spent half of elementary school feeling like a visitor from another world—until she'd found Cy and Bina and Nick, who seemed to have come from that other world too.

And now she'd lost them again.

She switched her laptop off. The room felt instantly emptier, as though someone who'd been sitting beside her had disappeared.

For a distraction, Fiona threw herself into unpacking her books. She started with her Macaulay collection—*Pyramid* and *Castle* and *Cathedral*—and then moved on to history and mythology. She was just organizing the mystery section when there came a long, low *creeeeak* from over her shoulder.

Fiona spun around.

No one was there.

Not in her room. Not in the hallway beyond.

But her door had swung a bit wider on its ancient hinges.

Air pressure, Fiona reminded herself. *Old wood swelling and shrinking.*

She stared at the door for several long seconds.

Finally, just to be sure, Fiona stepped through the door into the hallway. She padded along the groaning floorboards toward the front of the house.

She peeped into her parents' new bedroom. A few things had already been unpacked: the jar of Cape Cod seashells, a rack of her mom's colorful pendants, her dad's collection of sneakers lined up in the open closet. The familiar things looked wrong in this new room, like they had been stolen from someplace else. Like even they knew they didn't belong here.

Fiona tiptoed toward Arden's bedroom door.

The door was shut but not latched, revealing a sliver of the room within. When they were little, Arden and Fiona had always kept their bedroom doors open, so the two of them and their shared books and toys could float easily from one room to the other. Now Arden and Fiona usually kept their doors closed.

With a toe, Fiona bumped the door wider.

She glanced around Arden's new room. Dozens of figure skating medals already dangled from the closet doorknobs. Awards and dried bouquets filled the shelves. Pictures of Arden hung everywhere: Arden jumping. Arden mid-spin. Arden waving to the crowd. Arden, Arden, Arden.

Fiona crept toward the closet. She lifted the topmost medal in the dangling bunch. It was gold, and heavy, with frilled metal edges and a blue-striped ribbon. This stupid little piece of metal was why Fiona was here right now, in this house, in this town. So that Arden could spend more time skating and win more stupid little pieces of metal.

Fiona stared down at the medal for another moment. Then she crossed the floor, crouched down, and slid it beneath Arden's bed. The darkness under the bed was thick. The mattress was low. With the dust ruffle in place, no one would spot the hidden medal at all.

A flutter of something that could have been excitement whirred to life in Fiona's chest.

She hadn't planned to do this. But it felt right.

Arden would find the medal eventually. She would wonder how it had ended up beneath her bed, and who or what could have moved it. Maybe she would wonder if this house was haunted. She might begin to wonder if she should have dragged everyone to this weird little town after all.

And that too felt perfectly right.

Fiona tiptoed back down the hall into her own bedroom.

The door creaked behind her once more.

This time, Fiona ignored it. She reached into a box and lifted out another heavy stack of books.

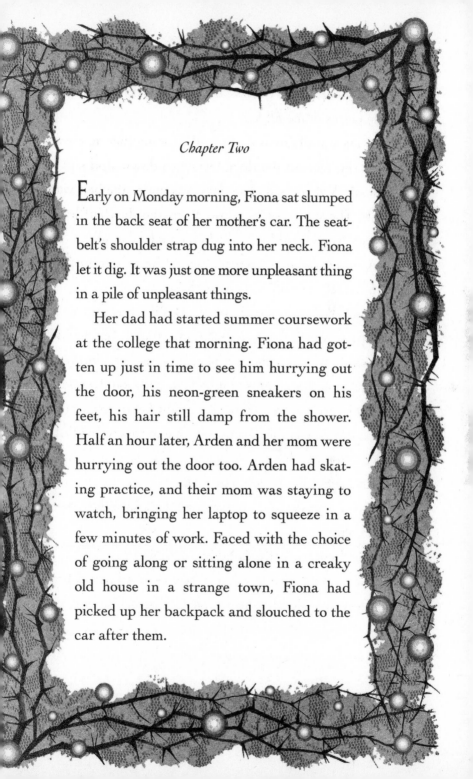

Chapter Two

Early on Monday morning, Fiona sat slumped in the back seat of her mother's car. The seatbelt's shoulder strap dug into her neck. Fiona let it dig. It was just one more unpleasant thing in a pile of unpleasant things.

Her dad had started summer coursework at the college that morning. Fiona had gotten up just in time to see him hurrying out the door, his neon-green sneakers on his feet, his hair still damp from the shower. Half an hour later, Arden and her mom were hurrying out the door too. Arden had skating practice, and their mom was staying to watch, bringing her laptop to squeeze in a few minutes of work. Faced with the choice of going along or sitting alone in a creaky old house in a strange town, Fiona had picked up her backpack and slouched to the car after them.

Arden sat in the passenger seat. Being thirteen made her officially old enough to ride in front, while Fiona was still confined to the back. It was just a couple of feet and a couple of years, but to Fiona, the gap between them felt like a chasm. She was stuck on one side, in the land of little kids, and Arden had leaped across to the other.

Slumping deeper into her seat, Fiona pulled the map of Lost Lake from her backpack pocket.

Maps lay at the intersection between facts and art— just the kind of spot that archeologist-historians liked to explore. Fiona had torn this particular map from a town guide that had been left on their front stoop by something called the Lost Lake Welcome Committee, along with a packet of coupons that said things like "Twenty percent off first dental cleaning!" and "Enjoy a bowl of oatmeal at the Perch Diner!" Fiona unfolded the map and studied its tiny print. Some of the street names were ordinary, like Main Street and Maple Street, but some were weird, like Chill Butter Brook Road, and Old Joyous Ridge Road, and Old Fitzwilliam-Fox Road. Now that she thought about it, a lot of the names started with "old." Old Turnpike Road. Old Minister's Road. Lost Lake was a town that really, really wanted you to know it was old.

"Weird," Fiona said aloud. "Old Hog Bristle Road."

"What about hog bristles?" asked her mom distractedly.

"There's a road here called Old Hog Bristle Road."

"Huh," said her mom.

Arden, who was looking at her phone, didn't say anything at all.

Arden had been allowed to get a smartphone for her thirteenth birthday. Fiona had a cell phone for emergencies, but it was basically just a calculator that could send texts.

"Wow," said Fiona. "There's a road called the Witches' Curve."

This time, nobody answered. Their mom turned from Lane's End Road onto Washington, and Arden went on staring at her phone.

Fiona slumped even lower.

"Why are you studying a map of the town?" Arden asked, after such a long pause that Fiona wasn't sure the question was addressed to her at all.

"Because it's interesting, first of all. And because we live here now." Fiona stopped herself before the words "because of you" could fly out too. "If you got lost somewhere in your own town, wouldn't you want to be able to find your way home?"

"I'd probably just use my phone," said Arden loftily.

Fiona stuffed the map back into her backpack. "How long is this practice going to take?"

"I've got off-ice class, then warm-up time, then my coaching session. Maybe four hours, if I practice my program for a while afterward."

"Four *hours*?" Fiona exploded.

"You knew it would be a long morning, Fiona," said her mom.

"Not *that* long."

"You can read, if you're bored," said Arden. "Or play games on Mom's phone. Or you could actually watch me skate. For once."

Fiona glared at the back of Arden's seat. "Let me out here."

Her mom caught her eyes in the rearview mirror. "Are you feeling carsick?"

"No. I just don't want to be stuck at an ice rink for hours and hours."

"Fiona." Her mom sighed. "You didn't want to stay home alone, remember?"

"I won't be at home. I'll be . . . here." Fiona glanced out the window at the town blurring past. "I can walk around."

"You can't just wander around an unfamiliar place."

"Why not?" Arden's voice was chilly now. "She's got her *map*."

Their mother sighed again.

They rolled along Old Mill Road, past a row of grand houses that lined the lake, all of them converted into law offices and dental practices now. Suddenly, beside the largest house of all, their mother veered to a stop.

"All right," she said, squinting through the windshield. "Here's the deal. You can stay at the library—*only* the library—while Arden and I are at the rink. We'll be back by twelve thirty. You have your phone with you, right?"

"Mom!" exclaimed Arden. "We're already going to be late!"

Their mom craned to face Fiona. "You can call me anytime. And remember your dad's campus is fifteen minutes away. You can reach him if there's an emergency. But I don't expect there to *be* any emergencies, because you're going to stay here, at the library. Right?"

"Right," said Fiona.

"We have to get going. Unless you're changing your mind again, Fiona."

"No." She pushed open her door. "I'm not changing my mind."

"See you at twelve thirty, ladybug."

Arden didn't say goodbye.

Fiona dragged her backpack out onto the sidewalk and listened as the car pulled away.

Before her stood a grand brick mansion. Tall, narrow windows glared down at the street from each of its three stories. A widow's walk fenced with iron spikes topped its steep black roof, and giant trees clustered close to its walls, cloaking the house in leafy shadows. CHISHOLM MEMORIAL LIBRARY, read a sign in the center of the lawn.

But this didn't look like a library.

This looked like a house that belonged to rich, strange, secretive people. The kind of people who might keep an insane relative shut up in the attic or collect tanks full of poisonous snakes.

Fiona ventured up the walkway to the porch. At the heavy double doors, she hesitated, wondering if she should knock and wait for a black-suited butler to let her in. But that was silly. This was a *library*. Besides, nobody had butlers anymore. Did they?

Fiona pushed one thick brass handle. The opening door pulled her into a wide, wood-floored foyer, where the air smelled reassuringly of books. Taking a deep breath, Fiona stepped through an archway into a room that was nearly as large as her entire house.

The room had parquet floors and damask wallpaper and tall, narrow windows bright with sunlight. It also had clusters of tables and heavy armchairs filled with gray-haired people. The gray-haired people all turned to stare at her. So did the librarian behind the broad wooden desk.

For a single, powerful heartbeat, Fiona wished that Arden was beside her.

Arden could belong anywhere. She seemed *right* no matter where she was. It had to do with the way she moved, as if she always knew where she was going and how she was going to get there. Fiona could tag along, unnoticed and unquestioned, because anyone who glanced at them would see that they were sisters. If Arden belonged somewhere, Fiona must belong there too.

Fiona took a breath, straightening her shoulders. She didn't need her sister to belong in a library. She could do this on her own.

Gradually, the gray-haired patrons returned to their newspapers and computer screens. The librarian, who was youngish, with olive skin and brown hair pinned up in a mound of swirls, gave Fiona a smile before going back to her work.

Fiona padded along the edge of the room, trying to ignore the glances that followed her.

All around the central reading room were doorways leading to other areas. STUDY, read a sign outside a bookcase-lined alcove with a brick fireplace. A long, rectangular chamber that might once have been a dining room was labeled REFERENCE. CHILDREN'S SECTION, said the sign outside a sunny glass room that had obviously been a conservatory. (*Just like in Clue!* Fiona thought.) And at one end of the central chamber, next to a sign reading FICTION—SECOND FLOOR, a broad wooden staircase angled upward.

Fiona climbed the steps.

A portrait of a white woman in a sea-green armchair hung above the landing. As Fiona drew nearer, she noticed that the woman was somewhere between middle-aged and old, with silvery-gold hair around her face, and fine lines around her eyes, and a triple strand of pearls around her neck. She wore a regal little smile—the kind of smile someone wears while saying, "This is mine, but you may use it." But the woman's eyes didn't match her smile. Fiona stopped on the landing, leaning closer. There was something in the woman's eyes that looked . . . was it *sad*? Or was it something else?

She was still trying to figure it out when a voice behind her said, "Margaret Chisholm."

Fiona whipped around.

Beside her stood another kid—the only one she'd seen in the library. His face was very round, and his hair was very pale. He looked about her age. Fiona felt a zap of nervousness. She wasn't good at talking to kids she didn't know. She either said too little, which made her seem unfriendly, or way too much, which made her seem weird. Why was this boy talking to her in the first place? And had he just called her *Margaret*? He must have mistaken her for someone else.

"Um—no," Fiona began. "My name is—"

"*That's* Margaret Chisholm," said the boy, nodding at the portrait. "She left her mansion to the town, so it could become the library."

"Oh," said Fiona, feeling stupid. Which was her least favorite thing to feel, especially in front of a stranger. "So she's . . ."

"Dead?" The boy glanced at the portrait. "Yep. A long time ago. But everybody who's from here knows about her."

The boy gave Fiona a look that lasted two seconds too long before jogging down the staircase.

Fiona rocked backward on her feet. The boy wasn't being friendly either. He was just telling her something he thought she should know. And not knowing it already meant that she *definitely* didn't belong here.

She turned back to the portrait. Fastened to the bottom of its frame was a little gold plaque reading OUR STORIES ARE WHAT BIND US TOGETHER. —M.C. Fiona glanced into the painting's eyes once more. Then she looked to either side, where the landing split into two parallel hallways overlooking the reading room, and scurried away to the right.

The hall led her past a row of rooms labeled POETRY and PLAYS and ROMANCE. And then, on the very last door: MYSTERY.

Fiona darted inside. She found herself in a wood-paneled room more than twice the size of her own bedroom. The floor was covered by antique Turkish rugs, and the ceiling was crossed by heavy beams and hung with antique glass lamps. It was the perfect spot to dive into a mystery novel. Especially because Fiona had it all to herself.

She trailed through the bookshelves, letting her fingertips bump along the books' spines. Most of them were covered with crinkly clear plastic. But suddenly Fiona's fingers hit something soft—something that felt like satin, or very cold skin.

Fiona halted. The book she'd touched was bound in dark green leather. There were no words on its spine, not even a little alphabetizing label. Fiona drew it out. The book looked old, like something you'd find in an antique shop, or buried in a trunk in an attic. On its cover, the words *The Lost One* were embossed above a sketch of a dark forest. Hidden in the forest's twisted branches were other shapes: hunched figures, things with wings, things with eyes.

Long Lost

Fiona plunked down on the floor between the shelves, her back braced against their solid wood, and opened the book.

Once there were two sisters who did everything together, it began. But only one of them disappeared.

A delightful little shiver ran down Fiona's arms. She held the book closer and read on.

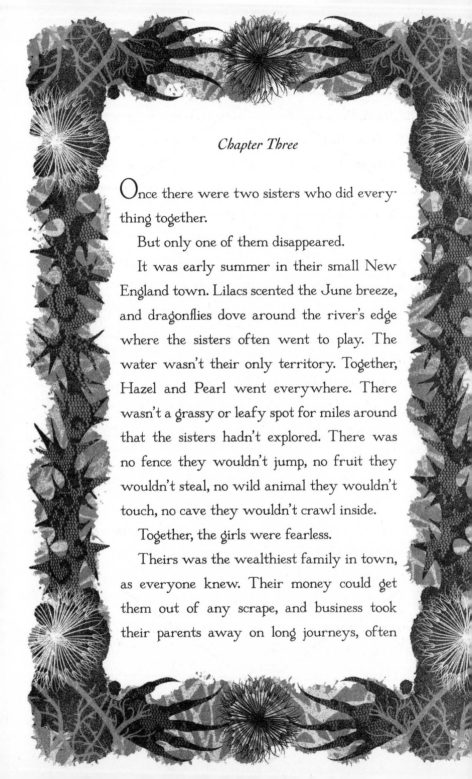

Chapter Three

Once there were two sisters who did everything together.

But only one of them disappeared.

It was early summer in their small New England town. Lilacs scented the June breeze, and dragonflies dove around the river's edge where the sisters often went to play. The water wasn't their only territory. Together, Hazel and Pearl went everywhere. There wasn't a grassy or leafy spot for miles around that the sisters hadn't explored. There was no fence they wouldn't jump, no fruit they wouldn't steal, no wild animal they wouldn't touch, no cave they wouldn't crawl inside.

Together, the girls were fearless.

Theirs was the wealthiest family in town, as everyone knew. Their money could get them out of any scrape, and business took their parents away on long journeys, often

for weeks at a time. In the summer, with no school to con-
tain them, the sisters had as much freedom as they could
snatch from their housekeeper's stern hands.

Their stuffier neighbors shook their heads. They tutted
to each other that those girls would come to a bad end.

None of them knew how right they were.

A gust of wind shook the tree outside the mystery
room windows, sending tiny fluttering shadows across
the open page. Fiona wriggled sideways into a beam of
sun.

She tried to picture herself doing forbidden things
with Arden, climbing over other people's fences, sneaking into hidden caves. Even in her imagination, Arden
wouldn't go along. She'd be too afraid of injuring her
skating ankles.

Fiona returned to the book.

One day, deep in the woods on the far side of the river,
Hazel descended from the top of a tall pine. She and Pearl
had discovered this ferny, emerald-green grove and chris-
tened it the Enchanted Forest. They had spent the spring
decking its trees with ribbons and silver bells that Hazel
had stolen from their mother's dressing room, and Pearl,
who liked to write and illustrate little stories, had filled a
notebook with tales set within its bounds.

Pixie, their shaggy terrier, hopped joyously around Hazel's legs as she leaped to the ground. He disliked it when Hazel went anywhere that he couldn't go, and up tall trees was at the top of this list.

"There, there, Pixie." Hazel rubbed his ear. "Good boy."

She had begun picking bits of sticky pine bark from her skirt when, from above, there came a terrified shriek.

Hazel's heart leaped to her throat. The shriek was Pearl's.

"Pearl!" she shouted. There was no reply.

For just an instant, Hazel's thoughts flew to the Searcher.

The Searcher was a dark being that skulked through these woods, awaiting the moment when it might catch another wanderer alone. According to the tales that wound through the town, any such unlucky wanderer was never seen again.

But Hazel knew that these were merely stories. And she was too smart for stories.

Besides, the shriek had come from above.

Hazel squinted up into the feathery green boughs. "Pearl!" she shouted again.

This time, there came an answering shout.

"Up here!" Pearl's voice was high and brittle. "I'm stuck! And I'm slipping!"

Hazel followed the voice to the base of a nearby pine, Pixie bounding along behind her. Through the branches, she caught a flash of lace-trimmed skirt and a glimpse of Pearl's small, worried face.

Hazel placed her hands on her hips. "How can you be both stuck and slipping?"

"Just HELP me!" A branch overhead shivered furiously.

With a sigh, Hazel pulled herself onto the lowest bough. Pine needles rippled around her, pointing like a million accusing fingers. At thirteen, Hazel sometimes felt like a grown-up, as though she should be responsible for both herself and eleven-year-old Pearl. But more often, she felt sure that she would never grow up at all. She climbed to the next bough, and the next. Pixie whined resentfully below.

"Hurry!" Pearl's voice urged.

Hazel climbed the rough rungs of the pine until at last, more than two dozen feet above the ground, her sister came fully into view.

Pearl hung from the tree, her hands locked around the branch above her head and her stiff-soled shoes balanced on a branch below. A thick swath of her brown hair was glued to the upper branch, sticking up from her head like the wick of a candle.

The sight nearly made Hazel laugh aloud.

"Hazel," Pearl gasped, as her elder sister climbed onto the branch below. "I can't hold on!"

Hazel took a calculating look. If Pearl let go of the branch above to grasp the sturdier one below, the swath of hair would be ripped straight out of her scalp. But if she lost her grip entirely, she would plummet through the branches, all the way to the distant ground.

"Why did you let your hair get wrapped around the tree like that?" Hazel asked. She drew herself onto Pearl's perch. The bough swayed, and Pearl's hands clenched tighter.

"I didn't *let* it." Pearl was too scared to sound truly angry, but Hazel saw her nostrils give their telltale flare. "It just *happened!*"

"Well, you shouldn't have let it happen," said Hazel, in her reasonable elder-sister tone, the tone that always made Pearl furious. "Don't move."

Hazel braced one arm against the pine's sticky trunk. Positioned between Pearl and the tree, she reached into her pocket.

"What are you doing?" Pearl whispered, as Hazel drew out her mother-of-pearl-handled pocketknife.

Not an appropriate toy for a young lady, their housekeeper, Mrs. Rawlins, had declared when Hazel bought the knife with her birthday money. But Hazel's mother had just smiled indulgently, and her father had laughed and said, *Let her do what she likes.* And so Hazel had kept it. It traveled with her everywhere: to the lake, to the woods, to church, slipped into a purse or pocket with lady-like discretion.

And it was not a toy.

"Just keep still," Hazel commanded. She gripped her sister's caught hair with one fist. Leaning against the trunk for balance, she sawed through the hair with the knife's sharp blade.

Set free, Pearl gasped, letting go of the branch above, her hands flying to the trunk instead.

"There." Hazel slipped the knife back into her pocket. "I'll climb down first."

Hazel descended the tree, branch by branch, making the final jump to the ground, where Pixie performed his joyous dance once more.

Pearl clambered behind, a bit more slowly. She hopped to the needle-matted ground. After a quick glance at her scraped palms, she patted the top of her head. The missing hair left a jagged tuft over Pearl's forehead, which stood out from the rest of her long tresses like a rent in silk. The tufty hair—and Pearl's stricken face—were so funny, Hazel couldn't hold back her laughter any longer.

Pearl stared at Hazel, her face darkening, the ends of her chopped-off hair twitching in the breeze.

"Oh, it's only hair," said Hazel, ceasing her laughter at last. "It will grow back."

"It will grow back in *months*," answered Pearl. "And I don't care about my silly hair, anyway."

"Then what's the matter?"

"Everyone will know." Pearl's eyes widened in exasperation. "They'll know I was climbing trees again. I'll be punished, and I can't pretend nothing happened, because the proof is right here on my head!"

"I was climbing too," said Hazel.

"But you can say that you had to, in order to save me. You'll be the heroine, and I'll be the bad one. Like always."

"Not like always," Hazel argued, although she knew Pearl's words held a kernel of truth. Hazel was craftier, cooler headed, and far better at pretending to be the well-behaved eldest daughter of an important family. Hazel missed as many curfews and tore as many stockings as Pearl, but she had more skill at hiding these transgressions. And she was far better at stitching the perfect lies to cover them.

"You know Mother and Father won't do anything," Hazel went on.

"Mrs. Rawlins will." Pearl's voice was strained. "I was already in trouble for stealing those berries from the Ephraims' garden. She said if I didn't behave for the rest of the summer, she would give Pixie away."

Hearing his name, the dog bumped his nose against Pearl's hand. Pearl rubbed him absently.

Hazel grabbed Pearl's other arm. "She can't get rid of Pixie, silly. He's ours. Father gave him to us. If Rawbones gets rid of Pixie, Father will get rid of *her*."

But the family couldn't do without Mrs. Rawlins, and they both knew it. If it weren't for Mrs. Rawlins running the house, it would fall into ruin in no time. In fact, the girls' father often said that without Mrs. Rawlins, they would all have died years ago of hunger, cold, or sheer dirtiness.

Pearl kept her eyes on the ground. Her face was such a mask of misery that Hazel couldn't stand it.

At last, with a sigh, Hazel pulled the knife from her pocket. She lifted a hank of her own hair and chopped straight through. "There."

Pearl stared at Hazel. Her mouth opened as though she was about to say something. The corners of her lips turned upward in the very beginning of a smile.

"Now when they ask us what happened," Hazel began, "we'll say that we were walking together in the woods, and we didn't look where we were going, and a branch covered with sap caught in our hair, so we had to cut ourselves free." She dropped the handful of hair to the ground.

Pixie snuffled at it. He let out a loud sneeze, sending up a burst of brown strands and rusty pine needles.

Hazel tucked the knife away. "Either we'll both get in

a little bit of trouble, or neither of us will get in trouble at all."

Pearl's smile widened, and Hazel knew that she had agreed. They would share the lie, half and half. They would keep yet another secret safely between them, one of them the lock, and one of them the key.

"Let's go," Hazel commanded. "We're going to be late for dinner as it is."

"All right," Pearl agreed. "But I'm not taking the shortcut."

The shortcut was a mossy fallen log that lay across a narrow point in the river. A person with good balance and little fear could climb across it, make a leap to a jut of exposed rocks, and jump from there to the other side.

Hazel's annoyance with her sister returned in a flash. "But it's so much faster!"

"The water's too high," Pearl argued. "Besides, Pixie is scared of it."

The dog whined softly.

"Fine," Hazel sighed. "We'll take Parson's Bridge. But you had better keep up."

The girls dashed through the woods, to Parson's Bridge, back to the edge of town, their shaggy dog bounding ahead of them. Behind them, the shadows stretched like the far larger, far more terrible secret that waited to wrap them both in its dark arms.

✦ ✦ ✦

That was the end of the chapter.

Fiona ran her fingertips down the page. She imagined Pearl and Hazel rushing across an old wooden bridge, their matching choppy hair floating on the wind. Arden would never cut off a hank of hair to save Fiona. She wouldn't let herself look less than perfect on the ice even if it saved Fiona from a year of groundings.

Somewhere in the mystery room, a floorboard creaked.

Fiona glanced up.

She couldn't see anyone, but a person could easily have been hidden by the bookshelves. Fiona listened. After a moment, she caught the creak of another step, and then a tired-sounding sigh, barely more than an exhalation.

Holding her backpack close, Fiona scooted around the end of the shelf, into the corner. She didn't feel like facing any more strangers. She huddled against the shelf, waiting.

But now there was only silence.

Fiona turned to the next chapter. If there was another breath, another creak, another pair of eyes watching her from somewhere in the room, she was soon too absorbed to notice.

Chapter Four

Everything changed when the carnival came to town, the book went on.

A train delivered the animals and acrobats, the striped tents that popped up at the edge of town like monstrous mushrooms, the carousel, and the wheezy calliope that sent tendrils of music through the summer air.

During its stay, Pearl and Hazel practically lived at the carnival. Pearl loved the tightrope walkers and trapeze performers. Hazel loved the trained bears and horses. She even befriended two young animal caretakers, a twin brother and sister named Mae and Matthew, whose father was the carnival's animal doctor.

The twins were fourteen, far closer to Hazel's age than Pearl's. They were bold and wild, quick to start trouble, and even quicker to run from it afterward. Pearl, smaller and slower, could not keep up. She could only watch as Hazel dashed off, seldom pausing to throw Pearl a backward glance.

Hazel and the twins pilfered fruit from the Millers' orchards without inviting Pearl along. They stole boats to fish in the lake, rowing away from the docks before Pearl could climb inside. More than once, they took a trio of carnival ponies for a ride on Joyous Ridge without even telling Pearl where they had gone.

Fiona stopped.

She knew just how Pearl must have felt: small. Unwanted. Excluded. A little like Fiona always felt while sitting alone in the back seat of the car.

And there was something else familiar about what she'd just read. Joyous Ridge. Had she heard that name somewhere before? Frowning slightly, she fell back into the story.

Late on the festival's last night, after the last call of the barkers and the final bow of the acrobats, after the grand lighted carousel had finished its very last spin, Hazel and Pearl watched the carnival close down.

They lingered on the meadow's cool grass, nibbling pop-corn from paper sacks as the starry sky grew darker, and the great striped tents billowed to the ground. The trained bears and the prancing ponies were marched onto waiting train cars. Roustabouts wound ropes and collapsed metal posts. Colored lights winked out.

Watching the carnival vanish made Pearl sad, although the thought that Mae and Matthew would leave with it lessened this sadness considerably. She glanced from Hazel's face to the deepening sky above. Pearl hadn't forgiven Hazel for the way she'd behaved all that week. And naturally, Hazel hadn't asked to be forgiven. She never did. But at least they were alone again, just the two of them.

It must have been nearing eleven o'clock, Pearl realized. Long past their nine o'clock curfew. Their mother and father were away at a gala in Hartford, but Mrs. Rawlins would be awake and waiting.

And she would be furious.

By now, she may have even sent Mr. Hobbes, the groundskeeper, out to search for them. Mr. Hobbes was more affable than Mrs. Rawlins, but his chattiness had its drawbacks. Come morning, half the neighbors and their household help would know that the sisters had disgraced the family once again.

"Hazel." Pearl nudged her sister's arm. "We had better get home."

Hazel's eyes didn't leave the vanishing circus. "Just wait. I want to stay until they're done. I have to say goodbye to Mae and Matthew."

Pearl felt a prickle of annoyance at waiting for Mae and Matthew, when they had certainly never waited for her. Still, she obeyed. She traced the constellations in the stars above. She folded her empty paper popcorn bag into a tight square, tapping her foot impatiently. Minutes slid by.

In all of those minutes, Hazel didn't speak to Pearl. She merely went on watching the roustabouts, waving at Matthew now and then when he looked up from his work and caught her eye.

At last a determination that had been forming inside of Pearl grew too solid to ignore.

She turned toward her sister. "I'm going home."

Hazel didn't give her a glance. "I told you to wait."

"I've *been* waiting. It's getting cold, and it's late, and we're going to be in enough trouble as it is."

Hazel lifted her chin. "Well, I'm not leaving."

"Fine," Pearl replied. "I'll go home alone."

Hazel's hand flashed out and grasped Pearl's arm. "You can't go alone. You'll tell Mrs. Rawlins everything."

"No, I won't."

"Just wait until I'm ready to go with you, and then I'll get us both out of trouble."

Pearl pulled back. "I'm tired of waiting for you. I'm tired of you always being the one who decides."

Hazel only grasped her tighter.

"Let go of me," Pearl demanded, her voice rising.

"I won't." Hazel's voice stayed low and dangerous. "Because you're acting like a silly little tattletale who wouldn't know what to do by herself anyway."

Pearl wrenched her arm free so suddenly that Hazel's fingernails left red tracks on her flesh. "I'm not going to do as you say anymore."

Hazel's eyes narrowed. "If you leave now, you'll be sorry."

After a week of other cruelties, Hazel's threat struck Pearl like a spark on dry tinder. Anger flared inside Pearl's chest.

"You'll be the one who's sorry." Pearl whirled around. She broke into a run, hoping to gain a head start.

But Hazel didn't follow.

Pearl dashed across the dark meadow, its grass trampled by hundreds of departed carnival-goers. The sounds of roustabouts at work and the brays of animals faded away behind her. She reached the edge of the meadow and turned onto the deserted curve of Turnpike Road.

Hazel was so sure of Pearl's loyalty. She was so sure Pearl would always be there, doing as she was told, tagging right behind. Well, perhaps Hazel was wrong.

Pearl raced along the wide dirt road. This late at night, there were no automobiles and no carts. Pearl was glad of this. No one would see her running alone down the road, far past the hour when young ladies should be safely in bed. But as the road wound into a grove, and the starry sky of the meadow vanished behind the fans of thickening trees, she grew less glad. And as she neared the rolling land of the cemetery, Pearl felt unhappier still.

She was not afraid of cemeteries. The town's cemetery was like a large private park, with tree-lined avenues and leafy nooks. She and Hazel had often gone there together, playing hide-and-seek among the headstones, picnicking on the family plots. They had even climbed to the roof of one mausoleum and taken turns leaping off onto the emerald moss.

But Pearl had never passed the place alone before, and not in the dark, so near midnight. She had always been with Hazel. And being with Hazel always made her twice as big and brave as she was on her own.

Pearl felt a flash of longing. If her sister were here, she wouldn't worry. She searched for the flame of her anger, hoping that it could strengthen her, but it had dulled with the lengthening distance from Hazel, like a coal pulled from a fire.

The cemetery gates loomed ahead.

Pearl ran faster.

Behind the stone arch and high iron bars, headstones gleamed a pale gray. Pearl didn't look at them as she passed. She kept her gaze fixed on the deserted road instead.

When the very corner of Pearl's eye spotted something moving at the edge of the cemetery grounds, she didn't look at that either. Looking would mean that she believed it was there, and she knew that it wasn't. She was imagining things. She was letting silly fears overtake her. And this was all Hazel's fault.

Pearl ran on.

Turnpike Road rambled past the cemetery, and then along the Millers' orchard and Edmund Crain's horse paddocks before reaching the edge of town. Pearl had some distance to go. She ought to come up with a plan in the meantime, something she could tell Mrs. Rawlins that would put everything right. But each time her thoughts began to coalesce, they were scattered by the sense that there was something behind her.

It was something black. It was something quiet. It was following her down a deserted road, still too far from the houses of town for anyone within them to hear.

Half-remembered stories filled Pearl's mind: tales of the Searcher whispered by Charlie Hobbes, the groundskeeper's son, the lore the older children traded around the Halloween bonfires, the warnings of a dozen housemaids. Once the Searcher found you, no one else ever would.

Now here she was, alone in the darkness. And this was Hazel's fault too.

Her shoes made quick, hard clops on the road. Her heart pounded harder still.

She had passed the Millers' orchard now. The paddocks lay ahead. If she could make it to the end of that fence, she'd be nearly to Rose Lane, and its little cottages would spring up around her. Next, she would cross Lilac Lane, and then she would be just a few streets from home.

If she could only run fast enough.

At the edge of her vision, the shadows flickered.

Something that may have been only a lock of her own hair, or that may have been the edge of a long black sleeve, trailed across the side of her neck. Pearl nearly screamed aloud.

There: the first cottage of Rose Lane stood just ahead, past Edmund Crain's barn. Pearl flew over the final yards, meeting the intersection of Turnpike Road and Rose Lane like a racer crossing a finish line. She glanced sideways, catching sight of her rushing reflection in the windows of the nearest cottage.

She hadn't imagined it after all.

There was something just behind her.

Chapter Five

Fiona gripped the book tight.

Years ago, on a trip to one of Arden's skating competitions, the Crane family had stayed at a hotel with a water park. Fiona had been too young to read the warning signs around the pools. She'd trusted Arden to read them for her. When Arden had pointed to part of one pool and said it was the shallow end, Fiona had hopped in.

She'd sunk straight through the water.

She hadn't expected it to close over her head, so she hadn't been holding her breath. She could still remember the terror she'd felt, with nothing to grasp or push off from—just that thick, silent water enveloping her like liquid glass, no air to scream with, and no one to hear her anyway. And then her dad's steady hands had dragged her back to the surface.

Of course Arden had been scolded. But she hadn't been punished. Not after she'd burst into tears that were even louder than Fiona's, anyway. Their mom and dad had had to calm Arden down, saying they knew it was all just an accident, that Arden would never hurt Fiona on purpose. Meanwhile, Fiona had glared at her sister across the turquoise water, her throat and eyes still burning, and almost wished that she *had* drowned. Because getting Arden into that much trouble might have been worth it.

Stupid Hazel, Fiona thought now, rushing on to the next page. If anything bad happened to Pearl, Fiona hoped the guilt would eat Hazel alive.

Pearl did not stop running.

The reflection in the cottage window was dim and blurred. She raced past too swiftly for a good look, but Pearl was certain of what she had seen: a dark, looming figure, far taller than she was, reaching out with one blackened, twisted hand.

She glanced over her shoulder.

The figure was no longer there.

Pearl felt no relief at this. It would be easy enough for something swift and silent and shadowy to dart behind a tree, and then to reemerge when she didn't expect it, snatching her up in those terrible hands.

Dashing to the other side of the empty road, Pearl veered again at the crossing of Turnpike Road and Oak Street, trying to make her course erratic enough to confuse any followers. Still, she could sense the Searcher's presence, the threat that could rear up anywhere.

Home waited around just one more corner. And there it was, its windows glowing with watchful lights.

Those lights had never looked so lovely to Pearl.

She leaped up the front steps, flew across the porch, and flung open the door. She slammed it again behind her.

Pixie, sprawled on the foyer rug, skittered onto his paws with a bark.

"Good heavens, child." Mrs. Rawlins appeared in the great room doorway. Like the lights of home, the housekeeper's big, broad-shouldered body and stern face had never appeared more welcoming to Pearl. "What can you be thinking, stampeding in here after—"

But she broke off with a good look at Pearl's face.

"There's something after me," Pearl gasped.

Without hesitation, Mrs. Rawlins grasped a tall silver candlestick from a nearby table and threw open the front door. Pixie lunged to the housekeeper's side, hackles rising, letting out a rumbling growl. Pearl scrambled backward.

Mrs. Rawlins examined the darkness. "What was after you, child?" She raised the candlestick like a club in one sturdy fist.

"It was—" Pearl managed. "It was the Searcher."

"The *Searcher*?" Mrs. Rawlins turned back toward Pearl, her expression shifting from concern to exaspera-tion. "Flying in here like a rabid creature, because of an old story? You've clearly scared yourself out of your own wits!"

She thumped the candlestick back into place and turned on Pearl with folded arms. Behind her, Pixie remained in the open doorway, huffing at the night air.

"And where is that sister of yours?" Mrs. Rawlins demanded.

"She was at the carnival, in the meadow," Pearl panted. "She didn't want to leave."

"So, you abandoned her and flounced off on your own?" Mrs. Rawlins's frown deepened as her voice rose. "I have two silly girls dashing around alone in the dark, hours past their curfew?" She shook her head furiously. "Charlie!"

The twelve-year-old boy who had been dozing in an armchair by the fireplace jerked upright.

"Charlie, go and fetch your father," Mrs. Rawlins ordered. "He's searching the woods along the lake. Tell him Miss Hazel is at the carnival."

Charlie nodded. He threw a half smile to Pearl, clapped his cap over his white-blond hair, and darted for the kitchen door.

Mrs. Rawlins returned her frown to Pearl. "You had better hope that your sister is safe, and that there *isn't* a spook from a silly old tale wandering around the town tonight."

"It *is* out there. I saw it," Pearl insisted. "And I tried to make Hazel come home with me hours ago, as soon as it got dark," she went on, stretching the truth to cover her disobedience. "She wouldn't. So I *had* to come home alone!"

"Leaving your sister, at night, with a crew of strangers and carnival types . . ." Mrs. Rawlins shook her head. "If your parents had any sense, they would give you both a good whipping, and then lock you indoors until you've gained some sense of your own."

"It wasn't my fault!" Pearl's voice crested in a shout. "It's Hazel's fault that I was alone out there in the dark and nearly got snatched by the Searcher!"

Mrs. Rawlins gazed down at Pearl from her considerable height. "Go up to your room immediately," she said, just as she had a thousand times before. "Get straight into bed. Pray that Mr. Hobbes brings Hazel home safe and sound, or you'll have abandoning your sister to add to your list of mistakes."

"But Hazel was—"

"Go on," Mrs. Rawlins commanded.

Pearl had known Mrs. Rawlins since the day she was

born. She knew each one of Mrs. Rawlins's frustrated, tired, and angry expressions, and she knew very well when there was no point in arguing.

She stomped toward the staircase.

Pixie didn't follow. The dog remained in the doorway, waiting for Hazel.

Pearl charged from the upper corridor onto the next flight of stairs. She and Hazel had rooms side by side at one end of the third floor. Mrs. Rawlins's rooms were at the other end of the hall, with a maid's chamber, storage for their mother's out-of-season clothes, and a bathroom in between. Pearl had always liked this privacy, the way the sisters' rooms were their own little realm. But now, the mere sight of her sister's bedroom door made her angry.

She had just endured the most terrible night of her entire life, and Hazel was to blame. Yet everyone was concerned for Hazel instead of her. Even Pixie had taken her sister's side.

Pearl stormed through her own bedroom door, locking it behind her.

It wasn't long before a fresh wave of noise filled the house. The sounds of Mrs. Rawlins scolding, and of Hazel's replies, first wheedling, then cagy, then stormy, rose all the way to the third floor, along with interjections from Mr. Hobbes and Pixie's happy barking.

The quick footsteps of a girl and the skittering paws of a dog pattered up the staircase to the third floor. A door opened and closed.

There was a moment of quiet.

Then, following a short, shuffling sound, a voice whispered clearly into Pearl's room.

"Pearl? Are you awake?"

Pearl, lying fully clothed in bed, turned toward it.

Hazel was speaking to her through their secret channel. Years before, Hazel had stolen a drill from Mr. Hobbes's tool chest and bored a small hole through the wall between their rooms. On Hazel's side, the hole was hidden by the edge of a framed picture. On Pearl's, it was shadowed by a chest of drawers. If there was light on either side, the girls could see straight through, and they could speak clearly without anyone overhearing, even when they'd been banished to their separate rooms.

Pearl had not turned on her bedroom light. If Hazel peered through the hole, she wouldn't see much but darkness.

"Pearl," Hazel's voice said again.

Pearl was still deciding on a reply when Hazel went on.

"What did you tell Mrs. Rawlins?"

Pearl sealed her lips.

"Did you tell her I made you run home by yourself? And did you tell her the Searcher had been chasing you?"

Hazel's voice was mocking, chastising, without any need for an answer. "This is why I told you to wait. Then none of this would have happened. I would have gotten us out of everything, and you wouldn't have scared your-self with some stupid old story."

Pearl swung her legs out of bed and stood up. The bed-springs creaked behind her.

"Pearl?" Hazel asked.

But Pearl still didn't speak. She crossed the room to the secret channel. Planting her feet, she dragged the heavy chest of drawers in front of the hole.

"Pearl," said Hazel's voice. But the voice was small and muffled now. It couldn't reach her, not well enough to push or pull.

Pearl crossed back to bed and threw herself down on top of the blankets. In a few minutes, she was asleep.

A muffled buzz came from Fiona's backpack.

She pulled out her phone. How could it be twelve eighteen already?

About to leave the rink, her mother had texted. See you in front of the library at 12:30.

Fiona squeezed the back half of the book, feeling how many pages remained. Definitely too many to read in the next ten minutes. And she didn't have a library card yet. She would have to leave without the book and come back to finish it tomorrow.

Or, Fiona thought, she *could* just take the book home. She could slide it into her backpack and smuggle it out without anyone ever knowing. When she'd finished reading it, she would bring it right back, exactly like you were supposed to do with library books—just minus the library card.

But second thoughts came swift and scary. What if she set off an alarm on the doors? What if the librarian searched her bag in front of all those staring people? What if she was never allowed inside the library again?

The thought of a library-less life clinched it. Fiona ran her fingers one last time over the book's soft leather cover. Then, stooping down, she wedged the book onto the end of the very bottom shelf, where hopefully no one else would find it before she came back. It wasn't like she had misshelved it, Fiona told herself. There was no alphabetizing tag on the book's spine. There wasn't even an author's name on the cover.

That was a little odd, Fiona realized. But there wasn't time to wonder about it right now.

Swinging her backpack over her shoulder, she hurried out of the mystery room and down the stairs to the circulation desk.

The librarian with the upswirled hair was bending over a stack of returns.

"Excuse me?" Fiona began.

The librarian turned. Up close, Fiona could see that her name tag read MS. MIRANDA. "Yes?"

"Is that your first name or your last name?" It wasn't the question Fiona had planned to ask, but it slipped out first. This happened to Fiona a lot. Her curiosity tended to bump everything else—caution, politeness, other thoughts—out of the way.

"It's my last name." The librarian gave a little smile. Her face was friendly. Friendly-ish, at least. Up close, the swoops and curls of her hair looked even more like magic to Fiona, who had never mastered a braid that didn't look like it had been chewed on by a grumpy cat. A small yellow shape was tucked into the curls above the librarian's ear. When Ms. Miranda stepped toward her, Fiona saw that it was a waving Lego man.

"Can I help you with something?" Ms. Miranda asked.

"Um . . . my family just moved here." Fiona's phone gave an impatient buzz. "What do I need to do to get a library card?"

Ms. Miranda's smile widened. "How old are you?"

"Eleven."

"You'll need a parent to come in with you. They'll

need ID and proof of your new address. Then we'll set you up."

"Okay." Fiona whirled toward the doors. "Thank you!"

She bolted out into the daylight and down the walkway to the waiting car. Behind her, the heavy library doors thumped shut, sealing the thousands of books and all their stories inside.

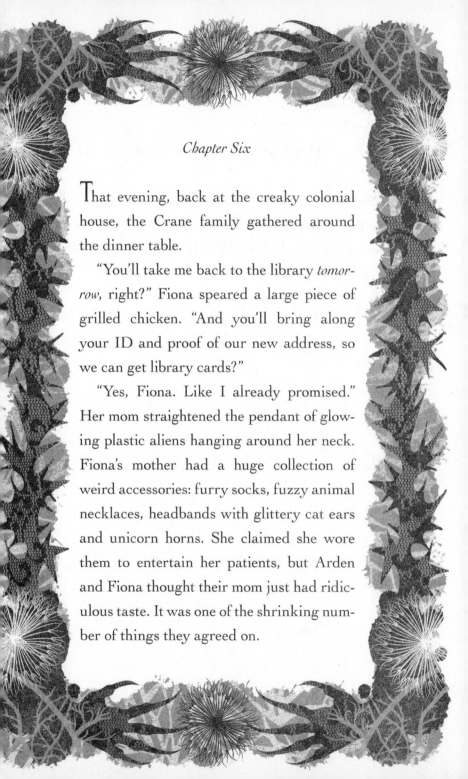

Chapter Six

That evening, back at the creaky colonial house, the Crane family gathered around the dinner table.

"You'll take me back to the library *tomorrow*, right?" Fiona speared a large piece of grilled chicken. "And you'll bring along your ID and proof of our new address, so we can get library cards?"

"Yes, Fiona. Like I already promised." Her mom straightened the pendant of glowing plastic aliens hanging around her neck. Fiona's mother had a huge collection of weird accessories: furry socks, fuzzy animal necklaces, headbands with glittery cat ears and unicorn horns. She claimed she wore them to entertain her patients, but Arden and Fiona thought their mom just had ridiculous taste. It was one of the shrinking number of things they agreed on.

Their mom smiled across the table at their dad. "How were your first classes?"

"Pretty smooth. We took care of all the busywork, looked over the syllabus—"

"Did you do any dissection yet?" Fiona asked, through a mouthful of rice.

"No, unfortunately." Her dad sighed, cutting a precise cube of chicken with the tip of his knife. "How was everybody else's day?"

"The drive to the rink feels like *nothing*," said Fiona's mom. "Sixteen minutes! We should have made this move years ago."

Fiona stiffened, mid-chew.

"Hey," said her dad, seeing the look on her face. "Now that we're all a little less busy, we could consider getting a dog again. What do you think?"

"I think yes!" Fiona shouted.

"I think we could talk about it." Her mom looked at Fiona, who was stuffing a shrub-sized bite of broccoli into her mouth. "Slow down, Fiona. The digestive system isn't a garbage disposal."

"I'm playing Kon-Struct with Nick and Bina and Cy at seven," said Fiona, with full cheeks. "We're starting a new city."

"I don't understand that game," Arden spoke up. "What's the point? It's just playing with blocks on a screen."

Fiona sat up straighter. "No, it isn't. It's engineering. And architecture. And it's the only thing I get to *do* with my friends now that we live *here*."

"Ew." Arden's forehead crinkled. "Keep your broccoli in your mouth once you've put it there."

"I *am*," said Fiona, wiping a fleck of green from her lips.

"What are your plans for the evening, Arden?" their dad broke in.

Arden's eyes brightened as they left Fiona's face. "Mom and I are going to watch that new dancing competition, *Never Before Seen*. The one where they have to pick their teams blindfolded, and then rehearse in the dark."

"That sounds *way* stupider than building with blocks on a screen," said Fiona.

Arden's frown slashed back toward her. "No it doesn't. 'Stupider' isn't even a word."

"Yes, it is," argued Fiona.

"I'm pretty sure it isn't," said their dad thoughtfully.

"I'm pretty sure it doesn't matter." Their mom reached for the pitcher. "Anyone else need more water?"

"So, what time can we go to the library?" Fiona asked as her mom refilled her glass. "It opens at nine. I want to be there right away."

"I've got to be at the clinic by eight thirty," said her mom. "Steven?"

"Dad's taking me to the rink tomorrow morning. Remember?" said Arden, with a sharp look at both parents. "I'm practicing for my next test. *Remember?*"

"Right." Their dad nodded, although he looked slightly surprised.

"Then who's going to help me get our library cards?" Fiona asked.

"Well," said her dad, "I guess I could take you to the library when I drop Arden off at home and head back to campus, although timing will be pretty tight . . ."

"But you promised!"

"I did?" Her dad looked surprised again.

"No. *I* did." Her mom sighed. "We'll get the library cards, ladybug. It just won't be first thing in the morning."

"But—"

"Oh my gosh," Arden interrupted. "It's a *library*. It's not going anywhere."

Fiona whirled toward her. "The book I want might go somewhere."

"Then pick another book."

"Why don't you pick another practice time?"

Arden's face pinched. "I *can't* pick another practice time. It isn't—"

"Enough," their mom cut in. "Who needs another piece of chicken?"

"I'm done," said Fiona, still frowning at Arden. "Can I be excused?"

After clearing her plate, Fiona hurried toward the stairs, leaving the sound of her family's voices behind.

Even with the hallway lamps shining, the old house was thick with shadows, holding pockets of darkness where light couldn't reach. The floorboards groaned under her feet.

Arden's skating bag hung over the newel post at the bottom of the steps.

Fiona froze beside it. Making sure no one else was in sight, she reached into the bag and drew out Arden's left skate.

Its white leather boot felt stiff and sturdy, nothing like the weathered cover of an old book. A purple skate guard covered the blade. A small knot was tied at the end of its lace.

Fiona knew why. At Arden's very first skating competition, the lace in her left boot had been a tiny bit too long. To shorten it, Arden had tied a knot near the end of the lace before soaring onto the ice and earning her first gold medal. Arden had tied a knot in her left lace, for luck, ever since.

Fiona worked her fingernails into the knot. It unwound, leaving nothing but a kinked spot in the lace. She slid the skate quickly back into the bag.

A thrill of secret power shot through her.

She hadn't really harmed anything, Fiona reassured herself. It's not like a little bit of knotted string was the key to Arden's success. Besides, Arden could retie the knot as soon as she noticed that it was undone. And, knowing perfectionist Arden, she *would* notice.

That was the whole point. Arden would notice, and she would wonder, and maybe she would worry. Just a tiny bit.

Smiling to herself, Fiona raced up to her own bedroom. She was just in time to join her friends for some Kon-Struct.

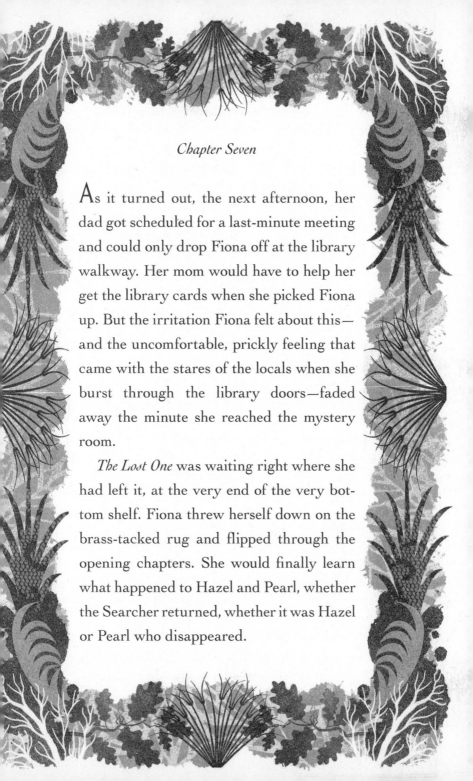

Chapter Seven

As it turned out, the next afternoon, her dad got scheduled for a last-minute meeting and could only drop Fiona off at the library walkway. Her mom would have to help her get the library cards when she picked Fiona up. But the irritation Fiona felt about this—and the uncomfortable, prickly feeling that came with the stares of the locals when she burst through the library doors—faded away the minute she reached the mystery room.

The Lost One was waiting right where she had left it, at the very end of the very bottom shelf. Fiona threw herself down on the brass-tacked rug and flipped through the opening chapters. She would finally learn what happened to Hazel and Pearl, whether the Searcher returned, whether it was Hazel or Pearl who disappeared.

Her hands twitched with anticipation as they found the right page.

The day after the carnival departed, a powerful thunderstorm struck the lakeside town.

Torrents of rain chilled the waters of the lake and pushed frothing waves against the riverbanks. Lightning struck an old oak at the meadow's edge, sending its split halves crashing to the wet ground. Edmund Crain's docile old horses spooked in their paddock, kicking down a fence rail and galloping off into the graveyard. And a group of young people who had been camping on the lakeshore fled, shaken and pale, to a local inn. It was not the storm that had rattled them, they insisted. It was the dark, towering figure they had seen watching them from amid the trees.

Naturally, Hazel and Pearl knew none of this.

They had spent the day apart, Pearl shut in her bedroom, Hazel rambling the woods, not exchanging a single word. They even took their dinners separately, Pearl with Mrs. Rawlins and Mrs. Fisher, the cook, in the kitchen, Hazel claiming a headache and withdrawing early to her room. By the time Pearl went up to bed, her sister's room was dark.

As quietly as she could, Pearl pulled the dresser away from the secret channel. But when she peered through the hole, ready to whisper Hazel's name, something about the silence on the other side pushed her back again. If Hazel still wouldn't apologize, Pearl wouldn't do the peacemaking for her. Fuming, she climbed into her own bed instead.

A few hours later, when the man and woman of the house returned from the gala in their chauffeured automobile, they found the girls in bed, thunder receding into the distance, and faithful Mrs. Rawlins waiting up for them with a pot of hot tea.

The grand house settled into silence.

But outside, on the second floor of the carriage house, young Charlie Hobbes lay awake.

The clamor of the storm had woken him, and something in the air, something heavy and watchful, refused to let him sleep again. He rolled onto his side to gaze out the window. And there, at the very edge of the lawn, he spied something moving through the trees.

It was tall; taller than any wild animal that made its home in those parts. Its body was dark and indistinct, and whatever face it had was concealed; by clothing or shadows, Charlie couldn't tell. It walked like a human, on two legs, and yet there was something inhuman about the scale of its body, the hunch of its head into its shoulders, and the way it moved, twitching, groping, then going perfectly still.

Charlie's lungs seemed to freeze.

He watched, breathless, as the dark shape trailed along

the yard's edge. It halted once more, staring up at the grand house.

Charlie blinked hard. The dark shape appeared to waver. Where before it had seemed solid, now it looked more like the emptiness between wind-shifted trees. Had his eyes been deceived by a shadow? As Charlie squinted at it, the shape seemed to dissolve into the woods, swallowed up by the darkness like a wet leaf sinking into a stream.

Many minutes passed before Charlie moved again. At last, overcome by exhaustion, he sagged back onto the pillow. Come morning, the memory of the dark shape seemed no more important than a dream, though it was one that remained, clear and strange, in his mind.

That is, until a nightmare took its place.

Fiona turned to the next chapter with an eager little shiver.

It was late the next afternoon when Mrs. Rawlins looked up from polishing the silver to glance out the kitchen windows. A serving spoon slipped from her hands and clattered to the floor.

As she would describe it to everyone later, Mrs. Rawlins's first thought was that she had seen a ghost.

The pale, fragile form drifting out from between the

trees with trancelike steps and haunted, hollow eyes barely looked alive at all. But as it tottered nearer, Mrs. Rawlins recognized the linen underdress that she herself had hemmed. And finally, beneath its blue pallor and stunned stare, she recognized Pearl's familiar face.

Mrs. Rawlins let out a scream.

The man and woman of the house were out paying calls, but in an instant, Mrs. Rawlins, Mrs. Fisher, and the housemaid had all rushed out onto the back lawn. Mrs. Fisher wrapped Pearl's bare limbs in a quilt. Mrs. Rawlins shouted for Mr. Hobbes and Charlie to leave the gardens and come quick.

Pearl was bundled inside.

The others clustered around as Mrs. Rawlins steered her to an armchair.

The girl was too cold even to shiver. Her hair hung wet and lank down her back. Mud clung to her shins. Scratches and scrapes covered her bare arms. Her eyes, when they chanced to meet anyone else's, would stare without focusing, as thoughtless as mirrors.

"Pearl!" Mrs. Rawlins shouted again and again. She shook the girl's chilled arm. "What happened? Did you fall into the river? Pearl?"

But Pearl did not, or could not, answer. Her unseeing eyes drifted past the housekeeper's face.

"Mrs. Fisher, run and fetch the doctor," commanded

Mrs. Rawlins. "Pearl, can you hear me? Pearl, what happened to you?"

At last Pearl's lips moved. "She . . ."

Mrs. Rawlins snatched up the word. "She what, child?"

"Gone," whispered Pearl, her gaze still floating above Mrs. Rawlins's head.

Mrs. Rawlins rocked back on her heels, the chill of terror sweeping through her. "Who is gone, child?"

Pearl's lips moved once more, but no word came out, only a sucked-in gasp. Her eyes glimmered with a spark of consciousness.

For the space of several heartbeats, no one moved.

"Hazel," Pearl breathed at last.

"Dear god," Mrs. Rawlins whispered. "Where, child? Where is Hazel now?"

"It took her." The glimmer in Pearl's eyes seemed to crystalize. "The Searcher."

Mrs. Rawlins blinked. "Pearl, where did you last see Hazel?"

"The Enchanted Kingdom," said Pearl dully. "Then . . . it came. It took her. And I ran. Into the water."

Mrs. Rawlins whirled toward Charlie and Mr. Hobbes, who stood beside her, working their caps in their hands. "Maybe there's a tramp or a wild animal out there," she told them. "You know where she means. That bit of old forest past Parson's Bridge. Go. Hurry."

Mr. Hobbes nodded. He grabbed Charlie by the shoulder and rushed him out the back door.

"Go from house to house," Mr. Hobbes told his son as they raced across the lawn. "Gather whoever you can and bring them along."

Charlie scrambled off.

With a coil of rope and an old rifle from the shed, Mr. Hobbes ran down the slope into the woods. Before long, Charlie came tearing after him, trailed by old Joseph Carlyle from across the street, the Morrisons' hired man, and the grocer, who'd been stopped mid-route on his cart. The hired man carried a cudgel. The grocer had his horse whip.

The group rushed through the trees.

"We'll check by the old mill first," Mr. Hobbes told the others. "Then we'll move downstream if—"

"Papa," Charlie interrupted. "Listen."

Everyone halted. From somewhere in the distance, across the river, there came the sound of a barking dog.

They raced across Parson's Bridge. The barking continued, high-pitched and panicked and growing closer. As they circled a knot of pines, the dog itself came into view.

Pixie darted back and forth at the river's edge. His curly fur was splattered with mud, his eyes fixed on something in the water. His barking didn't cease as the men raced closer.

65

Mr. Hobbes scanned the scene. The water narrowed here, running fast and deep before twisting and widening in its course to the lake. A few fallen trees lay in the waves, the tips of their branches nearly reaching from one side to the other. On the bank, trammeled by the dog's pacing paws, were multiple sets of shoe prints. Pixie's frenzied tracks had erased any chance of reading those prints, deciphering how many feet had made them, or where those feet had gone.

"Papa," Charlie murmured again. He nudged his father's arm.

Mr. Hobbes turned to follow the boy's gaze.

Nearly halfway across the water, caught in a cluster of branches, was something pale and soft. Something that rippled on the waves.

The group moved fast. The hired man stayed on the bank, holding one end of the rope. The rest pulled the rope into the waves, Charlie stopping where the water was ankle-deep, Mr. Carlyle and the grocer wading farther. Mr. Hobbes, with the rope's far end tied around his waist, strode and then swam past them all, into the rain-swollen river.

The dog's hoarse barks accelerated.

Mr. Hobbes reached the heap of fabric.

There was nothing inside of it.

It was only an empty dress: an empty, linen, lace-edged

dress, which belonged, as Mr. Hobbes and Charlie recognized, not to Hazel, but to Pearl.

When Mr. Hobbes returned to the bank with the dripping dress over his arm, Pixie finally fell silent. The dog buried his nose in the dress. Then he turned, seemingly confused, to sniff along the bank once more.

"Pixie," Charlie called, but the dog had resumed his frantic pacing, searching for something no one else could sense.

Before long, the woods were filled with sheriff's deputies, neighbors, curious onlookers. They searched for hours, wading in the river, checking the ruined mill, examining each hole and hillside, until darkness settled over everything like a cold fog. At last, when even the brightest lanterns became useless, the whole company trudged back to town.

Mr. Hobbes carried Pearl's sodden dress. Charlie led Pixie, whose collar was tied to the length of rope, and who whined and pulled backward the entire way.

Meanwhile, inside the grand house, Hazel's father was telephoning important friends, gathering more help. Hazel's mother was shut in her bedroom. Pearl sat, as still as a plaster mannequin, in a chair near the fire. When anyone questioned her, whether it was her father, the priest, or the sheriff himself, she would say nothing but what she had said before.

The Searcher took her sister.

And now she was gone.

Fiona didn't even notice when her phone began to ring.

It had just buzzed for the eighth or ninth time, and Fiona was hoping that whatever was making that annoying sound would knock it off, when she realized the noise was coming from her own backpack.

"Fiona?" said her mom's voice, when Fiona finally answered. "I'm on my way to the library right now. I'll need you to meet me outside."

"But—" Fiona glanced at the phone's clock. "You're not supposed to come for another hour!"

"I know. Arden's evening dance class was cancelled without us getting notified, so she's waiting outside the studio right now. She walked straight there from the rink, and the doors are locked. We can't just leave her standing on the street."

Fiona was pretty sure they *could*. "Can't you go get Arden by yourself, and pick me up when you come back?"

"I have two errands to do on the way home. By the time we get back to Lost Lake, the library will be long closed. I'm sorry, ladybug."

"Wait," said Fiona. "You were supposed to come

inside and help me get a library card!"

"I know." Her mom's voice was gentle. "We'll just have to do it another time. I'll see you in three minutes."

The call cut off.

Fiona would have liked to throw something, or slam a heavy door, but she was in the last place where a person should do those things. Instead, fuming, she shoved *The Lost One* back into its spot at the end of the bottom row. Then she stalked down the steps, past the stares of the strangers in the reading room, and out the library doors.

Her mom craned around with an apologetic smile as Fiona threw herself into the back seat. "I am really sorry about the change of plans, ladybug. It wasn't my idea, believe me."

Fiona nodded but didn't answer.

Her mom steered back onto the quiet street. "I'm glad you're enjoying the library so much."

"I'd enjoy it more if I had a library card," Fiona mumbled, low enough that her mom might not hear.

They rolled along Old Mill Road and turned right onto Old Turnpike, leaving the library behind. Through her window, Fiona watched downtown Lost Lake slide past, its outlines blurring like a photograph dipped in water. There went another steepled white church. There went a row of cozy little cottages. There went a crooked street sign reading ROSE LANE.

Rose Lane. Fiona shifted in her seat. Hadn't she just heard that name somewhere?

"Hey." Her mom's voice snipped through her thoughts. "How about I take you to the library the minute I get home from work tomorrow, and we both get our library cards?"

"The *minute* you get home?"

"Yes. I promise. And how about if you get to choose what we do for dinner tonight?"

Fiona met her mom's eyes in the rearview mirror and gave her the start of a smile. "That sounds good."

They drove on, past sagging wooden fences and ancient overgrown orchards, past a silent cemetery and a small patch of meadow that stood against the surrounding forest. But Fiona wasn't looking out her window anymore.

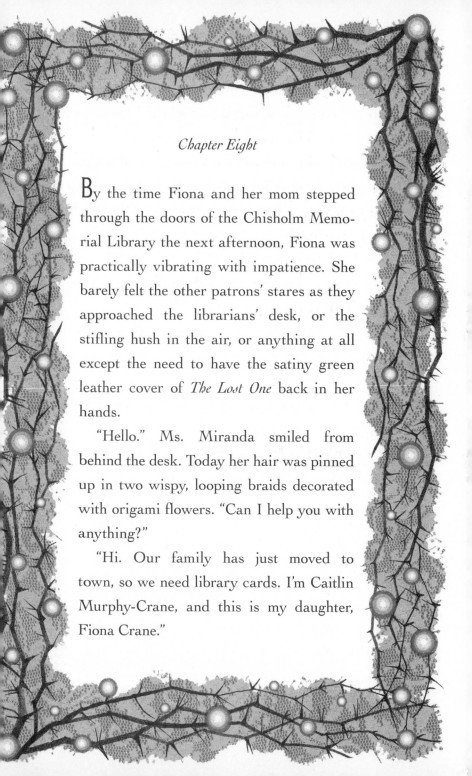

Chapter Eight

By the time Fiona and her mom stepped through the doors of the Chisholm Memorial Library the next afternoon, Fiona was practically vibrating with impatience. She barely felt the other patrons' stares as they approached the librarians' desk, or the stifling hush in the air, or anything at all except the need to have the satiny green leather cover of *The Lost One* back in her hands.

"Hello." Ms. Miranda smiled from behind the desk. Today her hair was pinned up in two wispy, looping braids decorated with origami flowers. "Can I help you with anything?"

"Hi. Our family has just moved to town, so we need library cards. I'm Caitlin Murphy-Crane, and this is my daughter, Fiona Crane."

Through the buzz of her impatience, Fiona felt a shift in the reading room atmosphere. She glanced over her shoulder. The room had grown even more still than usual. All the people in the nearby chairs had turned toward the circulation desk. A knot of three old men at the newspaper rack had dropped their murmured conversation to listen.

Ms. Miranda ignored all of this. "Welcome to Lost Lake." Her bright brown eyes flicked to Fiona. "I've seen you in here already, haven't I?"

Fiona could have sworn everyone else in the room leaned closer. She nodded, keeping a wordy answer inside.

"It's a beautiful old town," said Fiona's mom, when Fiona didn't speak. "And this is a *beautiful* old building."

"Yes. The Chisholm house," said Ms. Miranda, rooting in a drawer. "We're really lucky to have it."

"The Chisholm house," Fiona's mom repeated. "Were the Chisholms town founders, or local politicians, or . . . ?"

"Frederick Chisholm was a very successful businessman," said Ms. Miranda. "He left the house to his daughter, and she left it to us."

"He was an *investor*." One of the old men spoke up. "Invested in a bunch of industries. Didn't make anything himself except money."

"And they weren't local," put in another. "Sure weren't town founders. Just moved here, built this house, and left again."

"Or died," said the third man.

Ms. Miranda's smile didn't waver, but Fiona saw it stiffen slightly. "This town is just *full* of history," she said, banging the drawer shut. "Can I see a photo ID, please?" She pointed at the chain of purple monkeys hanging around Ms. Murphy-Crane's neck. "Love your necklace, by the way."

Fiona rocked from foot to foot while her mother dug for her wallet. She could practically feel *The Lost One*'s pages between her fingers already. She would flip through them until she found Pearl, soaked and shaken, staggering back to her house, and then—

"Fiona?" Her mom gave her a look. "Do you need to use the restroom?"

"No." Fiona stopped rocking. "I'm just excited."

"Almost finished." Ms. Miranda slid two plastic cards across the countertop. "All I need now is a signature."

Fiona grabbed her card. *Chisholm Memorial Library*, read the text beneath a sketch of the big brick building, widow's walk and looming trees and all.

The other new things that had been shoved into her life hadn't been hers to choose. But this new library card was different. She *wanted* it, even if it would mean that she truly lived in this strange, whispery old town.

She signed her name on the bare black line. *Fiona Crane.*

"Arden and I are heading to Framingham to pick up her new costume," said her mom, dropping her own library card into her bag. "Your dad will pick you up at twenty to six. Fiona, are you listening?"

"Twenty to six," said Fiona, sidling toward the staircase.

Her mom laughed. "See you later, ladybug. Happy reading."

Fifteen seconds later, Fiona was skidding through the door of the mystery room. Late afternoon sun gilded the paneled walls. The rows of waiting books seemed to glow. In the back corner, Fiona threw herself down on the rug, yanked the book from the very end of the very bottom shelf, and settled into reading position, shivering with happy anticipation. She flipped the book open in her lap.

And immediately closed it again.

This was the wrong book.

Fiona rocked back, frowning. This book had a crinkly cellophane cover and a painting of a thatched cottage on the front. *A Quiet Country Murder,* by Rebecca Zales. Fiona shoved it back into place. On her hands and knees, she scanned the rest of the shelf. A row of ordinary, shiny spines stared back at her.

Fiona shot to her feet. Someone must have reshelved the book. Maybe *The Lost One* was back in the spot where she'd discovered it in the first place.

She darted through the rows. There was no sign of *The Lost One* on the shelf where she'd found it. Or on the next shelf. Or the next.

Fiona's heart tripped. She forced herself to walk slowly along each shelf once more, trailing her eyes and her fingertips over every book.

The Lost One wasn't there. It wasn't anywhere.

Fiona raced back along the upper corridor, down the staircase, and through the central room so quickly that the newspapers in their racks fluttered like paper wings.

"Where's the fire?" called one old man.

Ms. Miranda glanced up as Fiona skidded toward the circulation desk. The paper flowers in her hair nodded.

"I'm looking for a book," Fiona panted, too desperate to care about the many eyes aimed at her back. "A mystery book. I started reading it here two days ago, but I had to leave it because I didn't have a library card yet, and now I can't find it."

"And you have to know what happens next. I understand *completely*," said Ms. Miranda. "Someone else may have checked it out, but we'll put a hold on it so you get it ASAP." She clicked a few buttons on her keyboard. "Title?"

"*The Lost One.*"

Something small and bright flickered in Ms. Miranda's eye—probably just light from the computer screen. "We have a recent mystery novel called *All the Lost Ones,*" she said, squinting at the monitor. "Is that what you mean?"

"No. *The Lost One.* I'm positive," said Fiona. "And this book was old. Like, at least fifty years old. It had a leather cover, and a drawing of a forest on the front. . . ."

Ms. Miranda took a quick breath through her nose. Fiona couldn't tell if it was a sniffle, or a gasp, or nothing at all. "Hmm. We definitely don't have a book by that title in our fiction collection." Her eyes flicked from the computer to Fiona. "Where did you say you found it?"

"It was in the mystery room. On the shelves."

"Well, that's very strange," said Ms. Miranda slowly. She typed something else, took a breath, and turned to Fiona once more. "I don't know what to tell you, except that the book didn't belong there." She gave a small, sympathetic smile. "I'd be happy to recommend another great mystery, if that's what you're into."

"No," blurted Fiona. "I mean—I *am*—but I need to get to the end of *this* one."

Ms. Miranda stared into her eyes for a beat. "I'm really sorry," she said. "Let me know if you change your mind about another book."

The sympathy on the librarian's face looked genuine. But that was no help to Fiona. Silently she turned away from the circulation desk, the stream of thoughts in her head sloshing so hard that it made her dizzy.

The Lost One hadn't been part of the library collection at all. Now it was gone. And she might never find it again. She'd never know what had happened to Hazel. She'd never know if the Searcher was real. She'd never know how it ended.

Fiona's eyes drifted across the central room, landing on the row of computers.

Wait a minute.

If you were looking for a book and couldn't find it in the library, a librarian would usually offer to get it for you from *another* library. Fiona had requested enough rare old books about Egyptian tombs and lost Mayan cities to be sure of this. But Ms. Miranda hadn't even offered. Why not? What would Fiona find if she searched for the book herself?

Fiona darted to a free computer. When she typed "The Lost One book" into the search bar, dozens of book covers appeared: lost boys and lost girls, lost lands and hearts and dogs, Lost Lake itself. Fiona scrolled through them all, page after page. But nothing was right. Maybe *that* was why Ms. Miranda hadn't offered to get the book somewhere else. Maybe she'd tried and couldn't find it either. Just in case, Fiona searched for "The Lost One novel." And "Lost One mystery." And "Lost One Hazel and Pearl." Still nothing.

But the book did exist, Fiona assured herself, fighting against the sinking feeling that pulled at her stomach like an open bathtub drain. She had held the book in her hands. She'd read half of it. She'd left it right where she could find it again.

If it had been there, and if it had moved away . . . then someone else had moved it.

What if that someone else—and the book itself—was still here?

Quickly, trying to make herself as small and silent as possible, Fiona circled the central reading room. She checked every desk and tabletop. She squinted at the books in other people's hands. Several people squinted back at her. A few of them even watched her suspiciously, as if *she* was the one who might have stolen something. But none of them had her book.

Fiona skulked through the study and the reference room next. There was no sign of *The Lost One* anywhere— although Fiona did spot the blond-haired, round-faced boy who'd told her about Margaret Chisholm, poring over a big book of maps. She scanned the upstairs rooms as fast as she could, rushing between the shelves until her vision blurred and her brain spun. But the book wasn't there.

Finally, out of places to look and almost out of time, Fiona threw herself down in one of the central room's big armchairs. She felt sad and annoyed and even a little sick, like she'd been about to dig into her first meal in days, and someone had whisked her plate away before she could take a bite.

If her mom hadn't come early yesterday, Fiona thought, she wouldn't have left the book behind. And her mom wouldn't have come early if it weren't for Arden's stupid dance class. All of this—like so much else—was Arden's fault.

Fiona bit her lower lip until her eyes watered.

And then, through the blur, she caught a flash of green.

It was exactly the right shade of green. It was the dark green leather of an old book. And it was sitting on a shelf behind the circulation desk.

The book hadn't been there when she talked to Ms. Miranda, Fiona was absolutely certain. The librarian must have found it for her after all.

Fiona shot to her feet.

She'd just taken a step toward the desk when all the library lights flashed.

"Library patrons, it is five fifty." The gray-haired librarian working beside Ms. Miranda announced into a small microphone. "The Chisholm Memorial Library will be closing in ten minutes. Please bring your materials to the checkout counter or to the return carts. Thank you."

Fiona halted, thrown off balance. Five fifty? She was already late to meet her dad. And a crowd of other people was hurrying to the desk before her.

Fiona rushed to join the line. She stood on her tiptoes, watching as Ms. Miranda turned around. The librarian's bright brown eyes slid over the checkout line, and Fiona craned even higher, waving a hand. But Ms. Miranda's gaze only slid away again. Fiona was sure the librarian had seen her—that there had been a moment when their eyes had met, and a knowing look had flashed across Ms. Miranda's face. But the librarian just turned, holding the green leather book close to her chest, and disappeared down a narrow hallway behind the circulation desk. The sign at the hall's entrance read STAFF ONLY.

Fiona rocked back on her heels.

It was *The Lost One*. It was *her* book. And Ms. Miranda was keeping it from her.

Why?

"Fifi!" said a familiar voice.

Fiona spun around.

Her dad stood behind her, looking exasperated. "Did you lose track of time?"

"Oh," said Fiona. "Sorry. I just have to—"

"We need to go," her dad interrupted. "We have to stop at the grocery store before it closes too. Come on."

Before Fiona could argue, he steered her toward the doors.

"Hey, Dad?" Fiona asked a half hour later, as the two of them picked through a box of spinach leaves at the kitchen sink. "Can you take me back to the library before your first class tomorrow?"

Her dad gave her a small sideways grin. "You really like that place, huh?"

"There's a book I couldn't check out that I *have* to finish reading."

"You're hooked." He nodded knowingly. "That's the danger of good books. They're a gateway to harder reading. One leads to another, and soon you'll be up all night, mainlining encyclopedias."

"I've done that," Fiona admitted.

"Yeah." Her dad sighed. "I think it might already be too late for you."

"What time will you be leaving tomorrow?" asked Arden from behind them. She was chopping strawberries for the salad into perfect heart-shaped slices.

"Around ten," said her dad. "Why do you ask, skater girl?"

"I don't have practice tomorrow. Maybe I'll come along."

Fiona spun toward her sister. "To the *library*?"

Arden shrugged. "It sounds better than being alone in this house for the whole day." She glanced around the kitchen, like it might be listening in. "It's kind of quiet and creaky at the same time, you know? It doesn't quite feel like it's *ours* yet."

"That's a great plan." Their dad smiled from one sister to the other. "You can keep each other company. We'll head to the library at—"

"*No,*" Fiona blurted, so loudly that the others stared at her like she'd just shoved a handful of spinach into her ear.

She couldn't have Arden at the library. Not now. Not when she was pursuing something complicated and odd and possibly forbidden, something Arden would never understand.

"I mean—you'd just get bored," Fiona faltered. "I can't keep you company. I need to find and finish this book, and I don't want any distractions."

"Fiona." Her dad blinked at her. "There's room for both of you in that giant library."

"Never mind," said Arden, before Fiona could speak

again. "I just thought it might be less boring than being here. If I knew it would be some huge *issue*, I wouldn't have suggested it at all." She turned away.

"Arden . . . ," said their dad.

"Never mind. Really." Arden swished out of the kitchen, leaving Fiona and her dad alone.

Fiona stared down at the spinach. Still, she couldn't help but notice the way her dad looked at her—like she was a specimen on a laboratory table, but one that he couldn't quite identify.

Chapter Nine

In myths, important gates were often blocked by guardians. Fiona had read enough folklore to know this. These guardians could be three-headed dogs, or hungry crocodiles, or angry bears with indigestion.

Apparently, in the real world, they could also be librarians with Wonder Woman figurines perched in their hair.

"Good morning!" Ms. Miranda looked up from the circulation desk as Fiona charged through the library doors. "Fiona Crane, right? New in town? Nice to see you back so soon!"

"Good morning," Fiona answered. She stepped to the desk, making her face and voice as innocent as she could. "I was wondering—did you find that book I was talking about? *The Lost One*? You said it wasn't in the collection, but I was thinking that maybe somebody just left it here, and maybe somebody *else* found it when they were picking up at the end of the night?"

Ms. Miranda's smile didn't waver. "I'm afraid you're still out of luck," she said. "And I know how annoying it is to leave a mystery half finished. Believe me."

"Okay." Fiona took a step backward. "Just thought I'd check. Thank you anyway."

Fiona turned her back on the circulation desk.

Sometimes the heroes of folklore had to use tricks, but they always found a way past the guardians eventually.

Fiona would do the same.

Taking a last glance at the STAFF ONLY hall, she sauntered casually toward the reference room.

The windows of the long rectangular room let in a green-gold haze of summer sunshine. A few strangers were seated at the big oak table, reading, making notes. They looked up as Fiona scurried by. Pretending not to notice, she browsed the tall bookshelves until she found something that looked interesting: a book about witch hunts in colonial New England. She turned around, gripping the book, and nearly smacked straight into someone else.

The boy with pale blond hair.

He frowned, leaning toward Fiona's face. "What are you doing here?" he whispered.

Fiona had already felt unwelcome. But now she *knew* she was. Because this was a strange question to ask someone who was clearly picking out books in a library.

"I was just looking for a book," Fiona whispered back.

The boy glanced down at the title in her hands. "You're interested in *local history*?"

"Yes," said Fiona, wondering why the boy said "local history" as though it was some kind of secret password. "I like history."

"I thought so," whispered the boy. Then, with another significant look at Fiona, he hurried away.

Fiona stood alone by the bookshelves as a wave of longing for her friends crashed through her. She and Bina and Cy and Nick were all a little bit odd, according to other kids at school. Most sixth-graders didn't pass notes in hieroglyphs or have their birthday parties at museums. But they were odd *together*. Here, she was odd and alone. And the only other kid she'd met so far was obviously going to leave her that way.

With the witch-trial book in her arms, Fiona crept back into the central room.

She found an armchair with a clear view of the circulation desk. Ms. Miranda and another librarian—a white woman in a plaid blouse, whose name tag read MRS. BREWER—were still there, looking very busy.

Fiona settled in the chair, put the open book in front

of her face, and stared sneakily over its edge at the librarians. She was just pretending to turn a page when her phone buzzed.

She fished it out of her backpack. A text from Cy glowed on the screen.

Two days until Operation Birthday (aka Best Birthday Ever)!

Fiona grinned, the loneliness wadded inside her loosening slightly. Can't wait, she typed back.

You and yr dad are meeting us in Springfield at 9:45, right? Then you'll get in the minivan and we'll head to Hartford!

Right, Fiona wrote back. I call a window seat!

Her phone buzzed again.

This is Bina. I'm stealing Cy's phone to tell you WE MISS YOU!!! And that Cy is going to lose this game of Catan.

Fiona's smile widened. Wish I was there. See you soon!!!!

As she slipped the phone into her backpack, she heard another phone ring.

Fiona scanned the room. Behind the circulation desk, Mrs. Brewer was lifting the receiver of the library phone, turning away from the room as she spoke. Ms. Miranda was gone. But gone where?

Fiona craned around in her armchair.

There—Ms. Miranda was disappearing through the doorway into the children's section.

This was it. This was her chance. And she had almost missed it.

While Mrs. Brewer's back was still turned, Fiona darted past the circulation desk and into the STAFF ONLY hall.

She hurried down the narrow corridor, heart thumping. To her left, she spotted an open coat closet, a door marked STAFF RESTROOM, and a heavier-looking door labeled STORAGE. Would Ms. Miranda have put the book in there? Fiona hesitated. Or would she have taken it to the very end of the hall, through the door with the frosted glass window that read OFFICE?

The soft glow of the glass drew Fiona onward.

She pressed her ear to the office door. No sounds came from the other side. She touched the knob and the door swung inward, its hinges wonderfully silent. Fiona slipped through, shutting it again behind her.

The office was wood paneled and windowless. From its size, Fiona wondered if it had once been a pantry, or one of those rooms where rich Victorians kept their china and silverware. There were three desks inside. And the cluttered one at the front had a name plate reading DIRECTOR—GRACE MIRANDA.

Fiona dove toward it.

She pawed through the piles of books on the desktop, in too much of a hurry to leave everything just the way it had been. Her heart seemed to stick to the roof of her mouth. She could feel its pulse in her back teeth.

And there, at the bottom of a stack of damaged novels, she found it.

The soft green cover. The sketch of the inky woods. *The Lost One.*

Fiona snatched it up, rubbing the green leather with her thumbs.

Ms. Miranda had pretended not to know anything about this book. But she'd obviously known where to find it. Then she'd sneaked it out of the collection and hidden it away, so Fiona couldn't get it back. But *why?*

Fiona would have to figure that out later. For now, she would put the book in her backpack and take it home, where she could read the rest of the story at last.

She unzipped her backpack.

"Ah-ha!" said a voice from the doorway behind her. "I *knew* you were in here."

And then the door thumped shut.

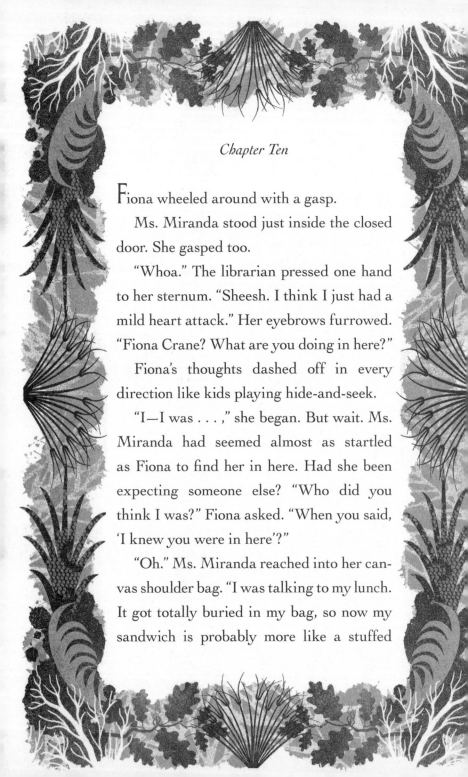

Chapter Ten

Fiona wheeled around with a gasp.

Ms. Miranda stood just inside the closed door. She gasped too.

"Whoa." The librarian pressed one hand to her sternum. "Sheesh. I think I just had a mild heart attack." Her eyebrows furrowed. "Fiona Crane? What are you doing in here?"

Fiona's thoughts dashed off in every direction like kids playing hide-and-seek.

"I—I was . . . ," she began. But wait. Ms. Miranda had seemed almost as startled as Fiona to find her in here. Had she been expecting someone else? "Who did you think I was?" Fiona asked. "When you said, 'I knew you were in here'?"

"Oh." Ms. Miranda reached into her canvas shoulder bag. "I was talking to my lunch. It got totally buried in my bag, so now my sandwich is probably more like a stuffed pancake." She pulled out a flattened brown sack. "Yep. Fabulous."

The thumping in Fiona's chest slowed just a bit.

But it sped up again a second later, when Ms. Miranda repeated, "What *are* you doing in here?" Her eyes flicked to the books on her desk. She stepped closer, and Fiona skittered out of the way, shoving *The Lost One* into the bag behind her back. "Did you get lost?"

"Not really." Fiona thought fast. "I know this area is marked staff only, but . . . I just think it's so interesting that this whole library used to be somebody's house. I wanted to explore a little more."

"Ah. I get it," said Ms. Miranda. "When you're interested in something, you have to find out *everything* about it. Right?"

"Right," said Fiona. How had Ms. Miranda guessed?

"I'm like that too. Needing answers. Loving to search for them." Ms. Miranda raised an eyebrow. "Have you ever thought about becoming a librarian?"

"I'm planning to be an archeologist," said Fiona. "Or a historian."

"Pretty close." Ms. Miranda perched on the edge of her desk. "So, you're interested in old houses, then? That makes sense."

"Yes," said Fiona, thinking, *Yes, it does! I came up with a perfect excuse without even trying!* "I think it's nice that

Margaret Chisholm donated her house to the town when she died."

"I do too." Ms. Miranda tossed the squished lunch bag onto the desk beside her. "The Chisholm family built a huge fortune and this huge house. Thanks to Margaret, we have this beautiful library."

"Did you know her?" Fiona asked. "Margaret Chisholm?"

"I never met her. But I think she's one of my best friends." Ms. Miranda gave Fiona a grin. "Margaret Chisholm died before I was even born, but spending every day in her house, handling her things, thinking about her wishes . . . it makes me *feel* like I know her. You know what I mean?"

The librarian's eyes coasted around the room, coming to rest once again on the stacks on her desk. When they returned to Fiona, her eyes seemed to carry something with them—something that might have been an accusation, if it had been said aloud. But Ms. Miranda didn't say it.

Fiona took another step toward the door. "So would this room have been a pantry or something?"

"Exactly," said Ms. Miranda. "This was the butler's pantry. And the big storage room next door was the kitchen."

"Well . . . thank you." Fiona took three more sidling

steps. She clutched her backpack, keeping it out of sight. "And I didn't mean to break the rules. I was just curious."

"Oh, I know," said Ms. Miranda. But her eyes were still sharp.

Fiona could feel them against her back as she blurted, "Goodbye," wheeled around, and bolted out the office door.

An hour later, shut safely inside her own bedroom, Fiona sat on her rumpled bedspread and pulled *The Lost One* out of her backpack.

She had never had a librarian stop her from reading before. There must have been a reason, something inside this book that Ms. Miranda didn't want her to see. And now Fiona would find it.

She riffled desperately through the pages to the spot where she'd left off.

Very, very late that night, the grand house and its grounds were quiet.

Quiet, but not asleep.

Lights still burned upstairs and down. Hazel's parents remained shut in the parlor with Father Carson. Mrs. Rawlins paced between the front and back doors like an aproned sentry. In her bedroom, Pearl lay with eyes closed, checked by the doctor and covered in soft blankets.

Charlie Hobbes had likewise been sent to bed. Although he'd climbed obediently up the steps of the carriage house, once again, he found it impossible to sleep. Instead, he lay staring at the ceiling, where a moth fluttered back and forth among the rafters, catching hints of the window's moonlight on its papery wings.

Gradually, the lights in the house went out, except in the parlor, where the adults kept their vigil. The sky darkened to inky black, strewn with a silver spray of stars. Charlie heard his father tread slowly up the stairs and throw himself into his own bed, his body heavy with the exhaustion of someone who hasn't found what he was searching for.

Still Charlie could not sleep.

He rolled toward the window. For a moment, he wondered whether he might be having the same dream as the night before.

Again, he spied a figure moving through the trees. But tonight the sky was clear, and a bright half-moon cast its glow over the lawn. By that glow, Charlie could see that the figure belonged to a girl in a trailing white nightdress.

Pearl.

Charlie sat up straight.

Pearl was far enough from the house to be concealed from its sight, surrounded by a knot of the largest oaks on the property. She moved strangely, bending and disappearing from his view again and again, as if she was struggling with something on the ground. Even from a distance, he could see her trembling. What could she be doing outside, alone, in the black of night?

Without disturbing his father, Charlie padded downstairs, slipped his feet into his boots, and hurried out the carriage-house door.

He headed toward the white glow of Pearl's nightgown. It fluttered in the distance, pallid and limp, like a broken-winged moth.

Could Pearl be sleepwalking? Charlie wondered as he approached. Had she wandered out here to search for her sister when everyone else had given up?

"Pearl!" he called softly.

His voice, muffled as it was, split the quiet of the night like a crack in glass.

Pearl spun around, her face stricken with terror.

Her feet were daubed with mud. The hem of her nightgown was heavy with dew. Before Charlie could get a look at what it held, her hand shot out from her side, flinging a small, dark object deeper into the trees.

"Pearl, what are you doing?"

Pearl stood as if frozen, her eyes wide, until he stepped closer.

"You frightened me," she told him. Her voice was faint.

"I'm sorry." Charlie glanced around for lurking figures in the dark, but he and Pearl were alone, as far as he could tell. "What are you doing out here by yourself?"

Pearl kept mum. Her eyes flickered away from Charlie's, catching glints of moonlight in their depths. Again, Charlie wondered if she might have been walking in her sleep, or if shock had clouded her mind.

"It's not safe," said Charlie at last. "In the morning, the crews will come back and search some more. I'm sure they'll find something. But for now, we should get you back to the house."

Pearl didn't move. Perhaps she could hear the uncertainty in his voice.

"It's my fault," she whispered at last, so softly that Charlie scarcely heard her.

"What's your fault?"

"That the Searcher took her. If we hadn't been arguing . . . if I hadn't turned away . . ."

"No," said Charlie. "It's not your fault. It's nobody's fault except for—for whoever did it."

Pearl gazed straight at him. "You don't believe in the Searcher anymore?"

"Well . . ." Charlie had told more than his share of Searcher stories. And he was nearly certain that he had seen a dark figure drifting through the trees last night. That hadn't been merely a campfire tale.

"You've seen it too, haven't you?" Pearl asked, almost as though she wanted the answer to be yes. As though that might reassure her. "In the trees?"

"I've seen something," Charlie admitted. But he needed to behave like a grown-up now, with Pearl looking so frail and strange. "I don't know what it was, though. It could have been just a shadow. And folks are saying there might be a tramp hiding out in the woods, or maybe an animal. . . ."

Pearl's glazed eyes slipped away. "I know what I saw."

A gust blew through the trees, making Charlie shiver. Pearl's nightgown billowed, but Pearl herself didn't stir, as though she couldn't feel the wind at all.

Charlie put out a hand. "Whatever it was, we should get inside now," he said, the words somewhere between a command and a plea. "Come on."

For another moment, Pearl kept still. Then, with one more look into the trees, she turned around and drifted toward the grand brick house.

Charlie followed her all the way to the back door. Only once she was safely inside and he'd heard the bolt hit the lock behind her did he stop to think.

He'd known Pearl most of his life and all of hers. She and Hazel had their secrets, and they were both good at concocting a story when it would save their skins . . . but Pearl had seemed so earnest tonight, and so genuinely afraid. Charlie glanced back toward the trees. What had she been doing out here? And what had she thrown into the woods?

Charlie scrambled back to the carriage house.

Armed with a lighted storm lantern, he retraced the steps he and Pearl had taken, following their footprints in the dewy grass. Then, keeping his eyes on the ground, he headed into the trees.

Something gleamed dully in the bracken to his right. Charlie lunged nearer. Lying on the ground was a small spade, one that his father used in the flowerbeds. This must have been what Pearl threw into the trees. Charlie picked it up. The blade was heavy with mud. What had Pearl dug up? Or what had she buried?

Raising the lantern, Charlie took a sharper look around. Nearby, at the base of the broadest oak of all, there was a disturbed spot in the soil. Charlie set down the lantern and began to dig. The earth had been patted roughly back into place, but it was still loose, and soft with recent rain.

Just inches below the surface, the spade struck some-thing—something as pale and delicate as bone, with a coat-ing that seemed to glimmer softly. Charlie stooped and grabbed it, rubbing away the dirt before lifting the item toward the light.

It was Hazel's mother-of-pearl-handled knife.

Charlie would have known it anywhere. He'd been there on the day when Hazel bought it, carrying it proudly home from Mason's Mercantile. He'd seen her use it a hundred times. She never went anywhere without it.

Why had Pearl buried it here? How had Pearl come to have it in the first place?

Charlie stood, wondering, in the flickering dimness.

He was sure of only two things: first, that Hazel would not have willingly gone anywhere without her knife. Second, that he couldn't keep it. Anyone found with the missing girl's favorite trinket would naturally become a suspect in her disappearance. He couldn't bring such a fate upon himself or his father.

Hurriedly, Charlie dropped the knife back into the hole. He buried it with the spade, tamping down the surface of the soil until only the slightest disturbance showed. He put the spade away in the garden shed. Then he returned to the carriage house, snuffed the lantern, and tiptoed back to his own bed, leaving Pearl's secret buried behind him, feeling strangely as though he was guilty of something far worse.

The chapter stopped there, but Fiona didn't. She was going to finish this book tonight, even if she had to do it while hiding under the covers with a flashlight.

She turned the page.

Losses never come alone.

Like wool unraveling stitch by stich, one loss brings

another, until even the most tightly woven fabric disintegrates into a heap of frayed threads.

So it was in the grand brick house after Hazel disappeared.

The girls' mother bolted herself in her bedroom, watched over by her maid and dosed by the doctor. In the study, with his telephone and a crystal decanter, their father did the same. Pixie seemed to develop magical powers befitting his name, escaping from knotted ropes and locked rooms to dash into the woods again and again, only to be brought back, whining and muddy, by unsuccessful searchers.

And Pearl became a living ghost.

She floated silently from room to room, occasionally drifting downstairs to appear, pale and mute, in the parlor. Mrs. Rawlins and Mrs. Fisher did their best to keep her fed, tutting over the plates that returned, barely touched, to the kitchen.

Worse still, night after night, long after doors were locked and lights were snuffed, Pearl was found wading along the edges of the river. Sometimes she was returned by Charlie and Mr. Hobbes, sometimes by a neighbor who had seen the nightdress-clad figure slipping through the trees. Afterward, no matter who asked, Pearl was never able to answer questions about what she had been doing in the water at night.

As the days passed, the grand brick house—

Fiona turned the page. But the next one was blank.

So was the one after that. And the one after that. All the way to the book's back cover.

Fiona flipped back to the middle of the book and pawed through the pages again, just in case she'd been imagining things.

She hadn't. The story cut off in the middle of a sentence, leaving all its mysteries unsolved.

Fiona riffled the handful of blank pages. She pinched the edge of one empty page and held it up to her bedside lamp. When she narrowed her eyes and leaned close, she thought that she saw *something* there—something that might have been print, but that was far too faint to read. Maybe it had been left by a typewriter that had run out of ink. Or maybe it had been erased.

Fiona tried rubbing the side of a pencil lead over a teeny part of the page, the way detectives in stories always did. But any impressions on the paper must have been far too small and delicate to uncover. All Fiona made was a smudge.

She slumped back on the bed, head spinning, frustration surging.

What was going on here? Was *The Lost One* so messed up and infuriating and *STUPID* that she would never learn the end of the story at all? Had she just stolen a book from a library *and* lied to a librarian—possibly the worst things Fiona had ever done—for *this?*

Fiona almost threw the book across the room, which might have been the third worst thing she had ever done, but she was interrupted by a tap at her bedroom door.

"Come in!" she growled.

Instead of her mom or dad telling her that it was time for dinner, the opening door revealed Arden, standing in the hall.

"Hi," said her sister.

Fiona shoved the book beneath her blankets. If there was anyone who *wouldn't* understand what was going on, it was Arden.

"What?" Fiona demanded. "Do you need something?"

"No." Arden seemed unfazed by her tone. "I was just . . ." She stepped into the room, leaving the sentence unfinished.

Fiona sat very still. Her sister hadn't set foot inside Fiona's bedroom since they'd moved. It felt strange having her there now, like an exotic animal had just opened the door and let itself in.

Arden gazed around, taking in the poster of Egypt's Valley of the Kings and the map of Sherlock Holmes's London, the bookshelves packed with mythology and history books.

"Your room looks nice," she said.

Fiona blinked. "Nice?"

"Like it did back home. I mean, it's nice to see all the same stuff here."

"It *doesn't* look like my room back home," said Fiona. "It's completely different."

Arden leaned against the bookshelf. She swept one pointed toe across the floor in an absent-minded ballet move. "I know. This whole house is different. That's why I like it that some things didn't change."

Fiona scowled.

Some things hadn't changed for Arden. She was still going to the same skating club she'd belonged to for years, seeing the same friends, doing the same things. But for the rest of the family—including the one whose room she'd sashayed into—there was nothing but loss.

"*Everything* has changed," she told her sister.

"I guess." Apparently, for once Arden didn't feel like arguing. She switched feet, now making floor circles with the other. "Hey. Does this house feel weird to you too?"

Fiona could have just said yes. Instead she asked cautiously, "What do you mean?"

"Just . . . this town, and everything in it—it's so *old*. I keep thinking about all the people who lived here before. Most of them must be dead by now, but . . . maybe their houses remember them." Arden stopped, running fingers through her glossy ponytail. "Never mind. It's silly."

Fiona studied her sister's face.

Arden was *scared*. This didn't happen often—mostly because Arden avoided anything that might scare her. She didn't like ghost stories or mystery novels. She refused to watch creepy movies. Of course, she had no problem leaping into the air on a pair of blades above a giant frozen floor in front of a huge crowd of strangers, but that was because Arden was a weirdo.

Seeing Arden looking jumpy and anxious was a rarity. It sent a pleased little ripple through Fiona's body.

Arden was scared? Good. It was her own fault.

"You're right." Fiona spoke up before Arden could back out. "I think places *do* remember things. I think this whole old town remembers things."

An idea flashed through Fiona's mind. She crossed her legs, settling back against the pillows. She was going to enjoy this.

"I've been researching the history of this town," she went on, placing her words like paint strokes. "There are stories about something that used to live in the woods nearby. Everyone called it the Searcher."

Arden folded her arms across her chest. "The Searcher?"

"Yeah. It was this tall, cloaked figure that lurked in the shadows. Every now and then, if somebody was out in the woods alone, the Searcher would grab them. And they would never be seen again."

Arden held herself tighter, as if she'd felt a sudden chill. "So it's, like, an old ghost story?"

"Nobody knows if the Searcher was a *ghost*, exactly. It might have just been a person in disguise. Or it might never have been human at all. It might have been . . . something else." Fiona let her words hang in the air, enjoying their whispery sound. And the look on her sister's face.

But Arden straightened up, tapping her fingers on the edge of Fiona's bookcase. "You know how stories like that get started, don't you?" she asked, her tone hardening into Big Sister Voice. "Somebody makes it up, because they need an excuse for something, or because they were confused or scared or stupid, and then they tell other people, and then all those people's imaginations start running away with them too. It's like when you learn a new word, and suddenly you start seeing that word everywhere." Arden gave a little smile, like she and Fiona shared a joke. "The word isn't actually following you everywhere. You're just noticing it."

"Right," said Fiona. "People *notice* things, once they know what to look for." She gave Arden a little smile back. "If you weren't *noticing* it, the Searcher would look like just another shadow in the woods."

Arden's smile wavered like a reflection on water. "Anyway . . . ," she said abruptly, turning toward the door. "I just wanted to see what you'd done with your room. If you want to come look at mine, you can."

"Maybe some other time." Fiona leaned farther back against the pillows. "I'm in the middle of a book."

"Sure," said Arden. "Whatever."

She glided out into the hallway.

Fiona grinned to herself. She could imagine Arden looking worriedly at the woods all around town from now on, keeping far away from any clusters of trees.

She pulled *The Lost One* out from under the covers and flipped through its ending one last time. The pages were as infuriatingly empty as ever, but there had to be more clues about this book to uncover. Maybe she would find them at the library tomorrow.

When Fiona fell asleep that night, it was with the book placed safely on the nightstand beside her.

And when she woke up in the morning, it was gone.

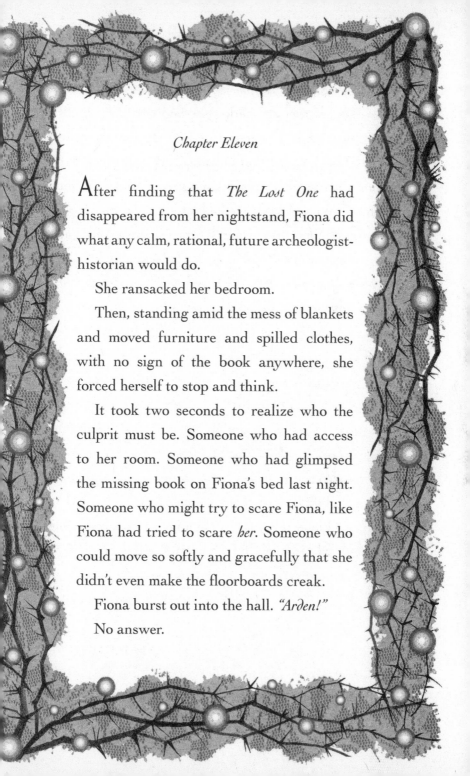

Chapter Eleven

After finding that *The Lost One* had disappeared from her nightstand, Fiona did what any calm, rational, future archeologist-historian would do.

She ransacked her bedroom.

Then, standing amid the mess of blankets and moved furniture and spilled clothes, with no sign of the book anywhere, she forced herself to stop and think.

It took two seconds to realize who the culprit must be. Someone who had access to her room. Someone who had glimpsed the missing book on Fiona's bed last night. Someone who might try to scare Fiona, like Fiona had tried to scare *her*. Someone who could move so softly and gracefully that she didn't even make the floorboards creak.

Fiona burst out into the hall. *"Arden!"*

No answer.

Fiona pounded along the hallway.

Arden's room was empty, the bed neatly made. She must have been at practice already. But her dozens of photos hanging on the walls seemed to be watching Fiona with smug, secretive smiles.

Fiona threw open her sister's closet door. She shoved the dangling costumes and dresses aside and rummaged through the boxes below. She threw back the perfect bedcovers. She yanked open the dresser and vanity drawers, spilling socks and leggings and hair ribbons and lip gloss and—

"Fiona?" Her dad's voice called from the staircase. "I'm heading to campus in ten minutes! Do you still want a ride to the library?"

Fiona froze, staring at the chaos she'd created. If Arden had hidden *The Lost One* somewhere in this room, she'd done a very crafty job. Then again, she might have taken the book to the rink with her, which would be even craftier. And crueler. And now, without even finding the book, Fiona had ten minutes to fix everything.

"I'll be right down!" she shouted back.

"All right. Ten minutes!" The stairs squeaked as her dad stepped away.

As fast as she could, Fiona threw the covers over the bed, rearranged toppled pillows, and stuffed wrinkled clothes back into drawers. Why did it always take four times as long to clean something up as it took to make a mess of it in the first place? It seemed like this must break one of the laws of physics. And unless Fiona took *eight* times as long, Arden would definitely notice that things were out of place.

But there wasn't time to be perfect. Not without missing her ride to the library. Besides, Fiona thought, looking at the wrinkly covers and not-quite-shut drawers, Arden deserved to have her perfect bedroom be a bit less perfect. A few small changes, like an untied boot lace and a hidden medal, could be creepier than something obvious. Maybe the room was perfect after all.

Leaving Arden's things almost—but not quite—repaired, Fiona hurried away.

Half an hour later, Fiona was hunched in an armchair in the central room of Chisholm Memorial Library, pretending to read *National Geographic* while glowering over the edge of the magazine at the circulation desk. She had planned to keep watch over Ms. Miranda today, to see if she could figure out what secrets the librarian was hiding, and why. But Ms. Miranda wasn't even there. Mrs. Brewer and a youngish man with dark skin and a blue bow tie were working behind the circulation desk. How much more frustrating could one morning get?

If only she had someone to sympathize. Someone who'd understand.

Fiona pulled the phone out of her backpack pocket.

Can't wait to see u all tomorrow, she texted Cy. So much weird stuff to tell u about!!!

She waited. There was no answer.

Sighing, she dropped the phone back into her bag. As she straightened up, her eyes coasted across the room, snagging on the portrait of Margaret Chisholm. Fiona frowned up at her regal little smile. OUR STORIES ARE WHAT BIND US TOGETHER—M.C. Sure. If you ever got to *finish* those stories.

"Hey," whispered a voice, so suddenly that Fiona wondered for a split second if the portrait was talking to her.

She jerked backward.

The blond-haired, round-faced boy was perched on the nearest armchair, staring at her.

"Oh. Hi," Fiona whispered back.

"Your name's Fiona Crane, right?"

Fiona blinked. "How did you know that?"

"It's a small town." The boy shrugged. "When somebody new moves here, everybody knows. And my family has lived here for generations, practically since Lost Lake was founded. So we know everything about everybody."

Fiona wriggled backward in her chair. This boy knowing more about her than she knew about him made her feel off-balance and small—like he was sitting at one end of a seesaw with bricks in his pockets, and she was trapped on the other end, dangling in midair.

Before she could ask any questions of her own, the boy plowed on. "Where do you live? Which street?"

"Lane's End Road," said Fiona slowly, wondering if it was safe to give a strange kid her address.

But the boy nodded like he knew this already. "South of town. Up against the woods." He nodded again. "My family lives on Church Street. So if you were heading into town from the north, you'd go down Old Turnpike Road, which used to just be called Turnpike Road. It goes past Wayfarer's Rest Cemetery." The boy leaned a bit closer. "Do you know where I mean?"

His skin was very pale, Fiona noticed. And his eyes held fragments of several shades of green. Their stare was bright and flickering, like a candle behind stained glass.

"I *think* I know where you mean," she said.

"And then, keeping on Turnpike Road, you'd cross *Rose Lane* and *Lilac Lane*." The boy whispered the names so emphatically, Fiona wondered if she was meant to whisper them back.

He went on staring at her with those intent eyes until she did.

"Rose Lane and Lilac Lane."

The boy nodded once more. *"Rose Lane."*

He gave Fiona a last, long, evaluating look. His eyes narrowed slightly, as if he wasn't sure what to think of her. Then, without saying goodbye, he stood and walked quickly away.

Fiona watched him go.

She couldn't wait to tell her friends about all of this tomorrow. She pictured herself and Nick and Bina and Cy bursting into the Hartford Science Center, poring over fossils, studying Egyptian artifacts . . . but even amid the happy pictures, the boy's words kept whispering in her head.

Rose Lane. Rose Lane. Where had she heard that name before?

On street signs on the way out of town, obviously, Fiona answered herself.

But that wasn't it. Or it wasn't all.

Fiona sat up straight.

There had been a Rose Lane in *The Lost One*.

Pearl had rushed across it with the Searcher chasing after her. And just before meeting the Searcher, she had passed an old cemetery. A cemetery on Turnpike Road.

Fiona's heart jolted in her chest.

She yanked a notebook out of her backpack. Rapidly, she scribbled down every location she could recall from *The Lost One*: Rose Lane. Turnpike Road. The cemetery. The meadow. The river and the lake. Parson's Bridge.

She stared at the list for a moment.

Then, backpack in hand, she dashed toward the circulation desk.

"Good morning," said the man with the bow tie as Fiona barreled closer. "Can I help—"

"Do you have any old maps of Lost Lake?" Fiona blurted. "Maps that would show the town back in ..." *The Lost One* mentioned cars and telephones, but it also had horse-drawn carts and girls who always wore dresses. "Maybe 1900 to 1920?"

The librarian's face brightened. Fiona had noticed that this often happened when you asked librarians for interesting things.

"Sure," he said. "They'd be in the reference collection, right over here."

Fiona followed him into the long rectangular room.

"Here's our local history section." The man, whose name tag read MR. OWENS, pulled a wide book from the shelves. "This is one of the most complete histories of Lost Lake. It has a lot of great illustrations, maps and charts and old photos. Sound like what you need?"

"That's perfect," said Fiona, already pulling the book out of his hands. "Thank you!"

She plunked down at the table and cracked the book open. Near the start was a series of maps. Lost Lake and Environs, 1700. Village of Lost Lake, 1776. Lost Lake, 1850. Lost Lake, 1910.

Perfect.

Fiona craned over the open page.

Rose Lane and Lilac Lane were small gray lines at the northern end of town. Running past them was Turnpike Road, lined by the big green plot of Wayfarer's Rest Cemetery. Fiona checked off the four items on her list, her fingers shaking with excitement. She traced Turnpike Road to the north, to another wide green space that had to be the meadow—and beside that, between a patch of woods and the river, was a narrow twisting track labeled Joyous Ridge.

Her heart thudded again.

She leaned over the book, her eyes like needles. There was the big blue body of Lost Lake, and winding upward from it was the blue line of the river. At one twist in the river was a black square labeled Lost Lake Mill Site. And not far from that square, so small that even Fiona's sharp eyes had missed it at first glance, was a little line spanning the river. The tiny letters beside the line spelled Parson's Bridge.

Fiona suppressed a happy squeak. She felt like an archeologist whose shovel had just scraped the wall of a buried city.

This was proof. *The Lost One* was set right here, in Lost Lake.

But what did that mean?

Fiona ran her fingers over the map. If the setting was real, was the rest of the book real too? Could the whole unfinished story—the story of Hazel and Pearl and the Searcher in the woods—be *true*?

She could think of one person who might know.

Fiona jumped up from the reference-room table.

She checked every corner of the library, peering into every room and behind every shelf, just like she had done for *The Lost One* itself.

But the blond boy had disappeared.

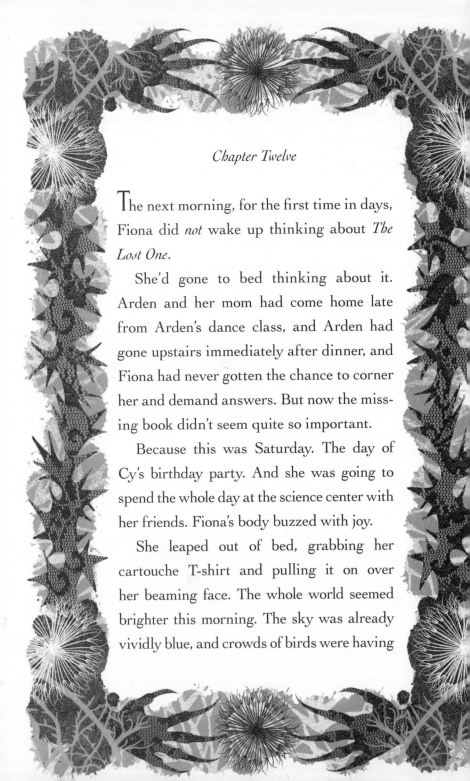

Chapter Twelve

The next morning, for the first time in days, Fiona did *not* wake up thinking about *The Lost One*.

She'd gone to bed thinking about it. Arden and her mom had come home late from Arden's dance class, and Arden had gone upstairs immediately after dinner, and Fiona had never gotten the chance to corner her and demand answers. But now the missing book didn't seem quite so important.

Because this was Saturday. The day of Cy's birthday party. And she was going to spend the whole day at the science center with her friends. Fiona's body buzzed with joy.

She leaped out of bed, grabbing her cartouche T-shirt and pulling it on over her beaming face. The whole world seemed brighter this morning. The sky was already vividly blue, and crowds of birds were having cheerful conversations in the woods outside her window.

Fiona had one leg inside her jeans and the other still tangled in her pajama pants when she noticed another sound.

Voices. Loud, familiar voices, coming from downstairs.

One voice wasn't just loud. It was shouting.

Fiona stepped out into the hall.

"I didn't write it on the calendar! *You* did!" Fiona heard Arden yell. "So I didn't know you had put it on the wrong day!"

Her mom and dad murmured something that Fiona couldn't catch.

"It was on the list Carolyn gave you!" Arden shouted as Fiona padded down the stairs. "I was *always* going to be skating on Saturday, not just on Sunday!"

"We get it, Arden," her mom answered. "It was a mistake. There's nothing we can do about it now."

Fiona slunk closer. Her family was in the kitchen, gathered around the calendar taped to the refrigerator. No one seemed to notice her hovering in the kitchen doorway.

Arden's face was warped with desperation. "Can't you just tell the clinic that you can't come in?"

"Arden, I have patients to see, and it's my very first week. I can't—"

"There's no other way." Fiona's dad broke in. "I'll cancel my meetings and take Arden instead."

"So Mom won't even be there?" Arden spun back toward her mom. "It's the Longfellow Open. One of the biggest competitions of the year. And you won't be there to see me do my new program for the very first time?"

"You know I'd be there if I possibly could." Her mom squeezed Arden's arm. "Now hurry and get your things, so your dad can still get you to the rink by nine."

Somewhere in the back of Fiona's head, an alarm began to clang.

"Wait," she said loudly. "Dad's driving me to Spring-field to meet up with the Kostas."

Her parents turned toward her. Her dad's face was a careful blank. Her mom covered her forehead with both hands.

"Fiona . . . ," she murmured.

"You didn't forget, did you?" Fiona fought the panic that began to rise through her ribs. "Because it's been on the calendar for *weeks*."

"No. We didn't forget," said her dad. "We've just got an amalgamation of issues here."

"But they're *Arden's* issues." Fiona kept her eyes away from her sister's face. Her sister, who had stolen her book and so much else. "It's Cy's birthday. They already bought me a ticket for the Egypt exhibit. You're sup-posed to drive me halfway there. You promised."

Arden made a noise like the start of a sob.

"Okay . . . let's look at all the elements," said her dad. "We can't change the fact that Arden has a competition in Boston that lasts all day, and she needs to have a parent with her. We can't change your mom's shift at the clinic, which means I'll be the one going to the city with Arden. We can't change the location or timing of Cy's birthday." He turned toward her mom. "Could the Kostas pick Fiona up here?"

"You want to ask them to drive two hours out of their way?" her mom asked. "And then drive *back* to Hartford?"

"I could take a cab," said Fiona desperately. "I'll pay for it myself."

"We're not sending you on a long-distance cab ride alone, Fiona." Her mom put a hand on her forehead again. "Girls, let the two of us talk for a minute."

Fiona and Arden stepped through the kitchen door and stopped in the hallway just outside.

Fiona stared straight down, her eyes so hot and her thoughts so furious she could practically feel them burning her toes. This couldn't happen. After days of loneliness, of waiting, of keeping this bright spot in front of her like a beacon, she couldn't have it stolen now. She glared at Arden from the corner of her eye.

At first Fiona thought Arden was just staring down at her own feet. But then she noticed two big tears dripping onto the hallway floor.

Arden's sock scuffed the drops away.

"Girls?" called their mom.

They darted back into the kitchen. And with just one look, Fiona knew. She knew from the way her parents were looking at her, not at Arden, with eyes that said, "We're sorry" and "We love you" and "Please be understanding" and a lot of other things that she didn't want to hear or see.

"Fifi," her dad began.

"No," said Fiona.

"If there were any other way—" said her mom.

"No," said Fiona, more loudly. "This isn't fair."

"You're right. It isn't," her mom agreed. "And we're so sorry. But Arden can't miss this competition. We just don't have another choice."

"We will make this up to you. We promise," her dad added. "We'll find another weekend when we can drive all the way to Pittsfield and pick everyone—"

"So I should just keep waiting and waiting, until *maybe, someday,* I can see my friends again?" Fiona broke in. "I didn't do anything wrong! I shouldn't be the one who gets punished!"

"It's not a punishment, Fiona. There's just no other option." Her mom spread her hands. "Arden's competition is—"

"NO!" yelled Fiona.

Her parents looked taken aback. Emotional explosions were Arden's terrain. Fiona was usually the quieter, sulkier, secretive one. But right now, Fiona's feelings were too huge to go anywhere but *out*.

"No!" she shouted. "I can't see my friends for a *single day*, a day I've been looking forward to *forever*, because you're choosing Arden over me?"

Her mother's face was like a broken china plate.

"Fifi . . . ," said her dad.

But Fiona had wheeled around and bolted out of the kitchen. She charged into the living room, threw herself down on the couch, and buried her head in the pillows.

She didn't want to cry. At least, she didn't want anyone to see her do it. She bit down on an upholstered cushion, muffling a scream.

A hand tapped her arm.

Fiona glared out between the pillows, expecting to see her mother. But it was Arden who sat beside her, perched on the edge of the coffee table.

"Hey," said her sister softly. "Fifi . . . I'm really sorry. About the birthday party."

Fiona stuffed her face back under the pillows.

"This isn't *my* fault either. I swear," Arden went on. "Mom and Dad were supposed to check the emails from the skating club to find out when I was scheduled to skate, but they read things wrong, or wrote them down wrong. It was a mistake. I'm sorry it's getting taken out on you."

Fiona didn't answer. Her throat clenched. Her lungs felt like two burning paper bags.

Arden kept still for a moment. Her fingers brushed Fiona's arm again.

"You know what?" said Arden, a ray of brightness filtering into her tone. "This isn't one hundred percent bad. Now you can come to the competition."

Fiona sat up so fast that the pillows around her tumbled to the floor. "I can come to your competition?"

Arden smiled at her obliviously. "To the Longfellow Open. You and Dad. It will be fun."

Fiona dug her hands into the couch cushions. She wished that her fingers were claws. She wished she had something big and valuable to tear into tiny bits.

"I thought that you stealing my book, the *one thing* I've found here that matters to me, was the worst thing you could do. But that was *nothing*."

"Your book?" Arden put on a confused look. "What—"

"This is all because of *you*." Fiona plowed on. "We had to move here because of you. I had to leave my friends because of you. Now I lose my one chance to see them because of you. And you want me to just come and cheer for you instead? 'Oh, Arden is so important and special and amazing that nobody around her even matters!'"

Arden stiffened. Her eyes turned hard. "Yes, I wanted you to come see me skate," she shot back. "Do you know how long it's been since you've come to *any* of my events? More than *two years*."

Fiona's mouth fell open. She would have argued, even if Arden was right—and Arden probably *was* right, because Fiona couldn't remember the last time she'd watched her sister skate. But Arden went on first.

"Do you know what that feels like?" Arden's voice was getting higher and louder. "When everybody else's families are there, supporting them, and my own sister never even shows up? Not at exhibitions, not at competitions, not even when I make it to regionals? Do you know how that feels?"

"No, I don't know how that feels!" Fiona yelled back. "I only know how it feels that no matter what I do or what I want, I'll always be less important than *my sister*!"

Fiona and Arden both shot to their feet.

Before Arden could beat her there, Fiona took off for the staircase. She raced through the hall, past her parents' stunned faces. She thundered up the stairs and bolted into her bedroom, slamming the door behind her.

When someone tapped at the door a few minutes later, Fiona didn't answer.

"Fiona?" her dad called gently. "I let the Kostas know what was going on. Everybody's really sorry to miss you."

Fiona kept still.

"Any chance you want to change your mind and come along with me and Arden?"

"*No.*"

There was a pause.

"All right," her dad said at last. "You can reach your mom at the clinic if you need to. Just stay home, and we'll see you tonight."

Again, Fiona didn't answer.

The hall creaked as he walked away.

Several seconds passed. Then the heavy bang of the front door echoed up the stairs, and the house went still.

Fiona lay on the bed, boiling in her skin. If she thought about Bina and Nick and Cy climbing into the Kostas' minivan together right now, the lump in her throat swelled so large that she could barely breathe.

Fiona shoved the tears out of her eyes. She couldn't just stay here, imagining everything she was missing, feeling miserable. She had to do *something*. Something that would distract her from the boiling, choking feelings. Maybe even something her parents wouldn't want her to do.

Well, they wouldn't know. And that was their fault, not hers.

Fiona yanked off her cartouche T-shirt and pulled on a plain green one instead. She stuffed the map of Lost Lake, her notebook, her phone, and her house key into her backpack. Downstairs, she gathered the rest of her equipment: a flashlight, a water bottle, a piece of sidewalk chalk. Then she headed to the garage for her bike.

Early on Saturday morning, the town of Lost Lake was even quieter than usual. Most businesses were closed for the day. Only a few cars rolled by as Fiona pedaled along Main Street.

She tugged out the map and pinned it against her handlebars. If she rode past the library to the bend in Old Mill Road, cut through the woods, and then followed the river northward to its narrowest point, she should find Parson's Bridge.

Beyond the library, at the end of the row of stolid old mansions, Fiona steered off the sidewalk. She pedaled across the lawn of a closed law firm and into the thick trees beyond. She hid her bike in a patch of ferns. Then, on foot, she hurried into the woods.

The ground quickly began to slope beneath her.

Fiona jogged downward, catching herself on low branches. Already she could hear the rushing sound of water. A few more steps through the lace of leaves, and the river sparkled into view.

It looked just like she'd imagined. The water was greenish silver and fast, sloshing along its rocky banks, and the woods were thick all around. Fiona wondered which of the towering trees had been here a hundred years ago. She pictured Hazel and Pearl walking beside her, the heels of their buttoned boots leaving matching prints in the earth. She imagined them breathing the same damp air.

If *The Lost One* had been set right here, there had to be some sort of hint to find. Some sign. Some trace. Something that could point her toward the missing ending. Spreading her arms for balance, Fiona hurried to the edge of the water.

She perched on a flat rock and looked around. To her right, the river widened before vanishing around a bend. And upriver, just a few yards away, there stood an old wooden bridge.

Parson's Bridge.

Invisible, icy fingers brushed the back of Fiona's neck.

She rushed along the bank and onto the bridge. The wooden boards thumped softly under her shoes, the river shushing and sparkling beneath.

The woods on the far side were dense. As Fiona stepped off the bridge, their shadows swept over her like gray silk, cool and light, covering everything. She dug through her backpack and pulled out the stick of chalk. With it, she drew a bumpy white X on a nearby tree trunk, just in case she needed to find her way back.

Fiona hiked onward, keeping the river beside her, marking trees as she went. The farther she walked, the quieter the woods became. It got easier and easier to imagine that this was the Lost Lake of a century ago— or the Lost Lake of a strange old book.

At last she reached a patch of forest where the pines grew tall and straight, and ferns and tiny white flowers caught the droplets of sunlight that slipped through their boughs. Fiona stopped and took a long look around. This could be the sisters' Enchanted Forest. Right now, Fiona could be standing on the spot where Hazel had disappeared.

Fiona turned in a slow circle, trying to observe everything at once, the way a researcher should. What might Pearl or Hazel have noticed, hidden among the ancient trees? What might they have seen? What might they have thought, but never had the chance to say?

And then, beside her, in the shadows, something stirred.

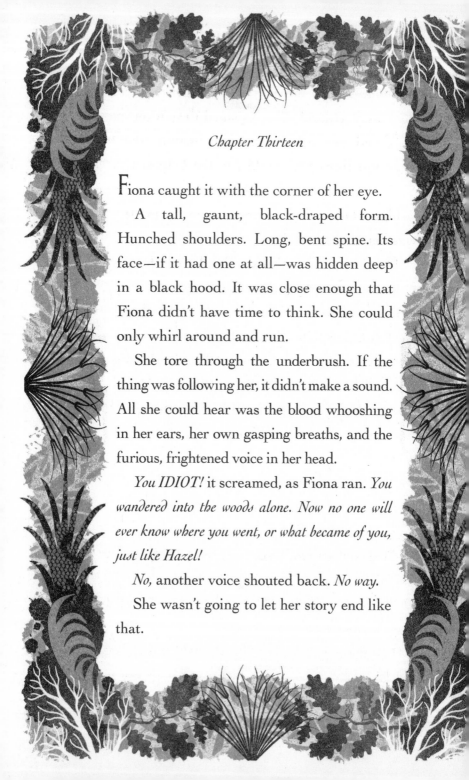

Chapter Thirteen

Fiona caught it with the corner of her eye.

A tall, gaunt, black-draped form. Hunched shoulders. Long, bent spine. Its face—if it had one at all—was hidden deep in a black hood. It was close enough that Fiona didn't have time to think. She could only whirl around and run.

She tore through the underbrush. If the thing was following her, it didn't make a sound. All she could hear was the blood whooshing in her ears, her own gasping breaths, and the furious, frightened voice in her head.

You IDIOT! it screamed, as Fiona ran. *You wandered into the woods alone. Now no one will ever know where you went, or what became of you, just like Hazel!*

No, another voice shouted back. *No way.*

She wasn't going to let her story end like that.

Fiona pushed her legs faster, farther, flying over the mossy ground. The Xs she'd drawn on the trees beckoned her on. In another instant, the woods began to thin. She could see the brightening glint of the river ahead, and the solid shape of Parson's Bridge waiting for her. She had nearly made it. This was her chance.

Planting her feet, Fiona whirled around.

There was nothing there. Nothing at all.

Of course there isn't, said a more reasonable voice in her head. *Because the Searcher doesn't exist.*

Fiona choked out a laugh. She'd probably been spooked by a strangely shaped shadow. Maybe she'd seen a black plastic garbage bag fluttering in a tree. Either way, there was nothing—

Snap.

A nearby twig broke.

In the underbrush, just a few feet away, the leaves began to sway.

Fiona's heart juddered. She took a backward step.

The brush rustled again.

"I know you're there!" she shouted, her voice breaking. "So *come out*!"

For one awful second, Fiona waited, wondering how the Searcher's hands would feel as they locked around her body.

And then, so fast that Fiona couldn't even scream, a dog burst out of the bushes.

It was medium-sized, with curly brown hair and whiskers that tufted beneath its nose like a mustache. Its eyes were black and glittering.

"Oh." All the air in Fiona's body whooshed out with that word. "Hello."

The dog watched her, keeping a slight distance.

"It's okay," Fiona told it, creeping closer. "Are you alone out here? Are you lost?"

She couldn't see a collar around its neck. But when Fiona got near enough to make sure, the dog skipped sideways—not like it was afraid of her, but like they were playing a game that Fiona hadn't joined yet.

"What are you doing out here?" Fiona asked it. "Were you following me?"

Abruptly, the dog bolted past her, galloping to the end of Parson's Bridge. There it stopped, looking back at her.

"And now you want me to follow *you*?" Fiona asked.

Of course the dog didn't answer. But it trotted across the bridge, looking back at Fiona with its bright black eyes.

She hurried after it. When she sped up, the dog sped up too. By the time they reached the trees on the other side, the dog was galloping. It led her through the woods, finally bounding up the slope and straight onto the back lawn of the library. Fiona watched, trying to keep up, as the dog neared the building. It stopped beside the back door, throwing Fiona one more look. Then it nudged the door with its nose and scampered inside.

After you've chased a strange dog through the woods and watched it sneak into a weird old library, you don't just stop there.

At least Fiona didn't.

She rushed through the back door after it.

The door opened into a small, empty chamber with more doors on three sides. To her right stood a set of wooden stairs. The sound of the dog's scrabbling paws floated down from above.

Trying to make the steps creak as little as possible, Fiona climbed after it.

The staircase ended in an alcove on the second-floor hallway. Over the banisters just ahead, Fiona could see the central reading room, the librarians and patrons going about their business below. No one seemed to have noticed the dog on the walkway above—the dog that was ducking under a STAFF ONLY sign in another alcove and scurrying up yet another flight of stairs.

Well, thought Fiona, she'd already disobeyed one sign. Besides, if she got caught, chasing a lost dog would be a good excuse.

She climbed under the sign and up the wooden staircase.

The library's third floor was hushed and dim. Unlike on the second floor, there was no open central chamber letting in light from every side. There was only a long corridor, stretching away in two directions, lined by a row of closed doors. Small windows at each end of the hall let in a few beams of daylight. The scents of an old house—aging wood, dust, and something smokier, like dead leaves—spun thickly in the air.

The dog had stopped at the end of the hall. It glanced at Fiona. Then it pawed at the base of a door, whining softly.

"What's wrong?" Fiona crept closer. "Are you trying to get inside?"

She reached for its shaggy fur, but the dog sidled quickly out of reach, whining again.

"All right," said Fiona. "I'll open it for you."

She turned the heavy brass knob.

The door groaned, swinging inward.

The dog bolted through.

Fiona froze on the threshold.

On the other side of the door was a bedroom. Not a

former bedroom, with an empty closet and dark spots on the wallpaper where pictures used to hang. A bedroom that looked as though it might have been used the night before.

If the night before was a century ago.

Fine lace curtains let in enough sun for Fiona to make out every detail. A high wooden bed with quilted silk blankets. A chest of drawers. A mirrored vanity, its top covered with treasures: a vase of birds' feathers, a chipped bowl full of agates, a silver hairbrush.

Feeling a little like she was stepping into a dream, Fiona ventured over the threshold.

She tugged open the vanity drawers. Inside were hair ribbons, pins, stacks of embroidered handkerchiefs. When Fiona lifted one from the top of its pile, she saw that the embroidered stitches were crooked, like someone young and impatient had been holding the needle. Between the cross-stitched flowers were two initials.

E.C.

E.C.?

Putting the handkerchief back, Fiona hurried to the closet. The stuffy smells of old fabric and cedar poured out as she opened the door. The closet was filled with hanging dresses. Antique dresses, trimmed with lace and ruffles. Dresses with pleats and pearl buttons.

Dresses just about the right size for someone Fiona's age.

The curly brown dog, which had been circling the room, darted into the open closet. It nosed at the clothes, snuffling loudly. The dresses swung on their hangers like dancing ghosts.

Fiona turned from the closet to the chest of drawers. On its top were more scattered objects. Fiona noticed a butterfly net, a sewing box, a few hairpins. And, behind them all, a photograph.

It was set in a little cardboard folder, the kind that you could close like an envelope or fold backward into a stand, the way it was folded now.

She picked it up.

In the grainy gray image, two girls stood side by side. They wore matching pleated dresses, matching buttoned boots, and matching floppy bows in their long hair. The face of the taller one was sharper, with a hint of a smile around the mouth. The shorter one's eyes were wider, dreamier, like she'd been looking past the photographer at something else.

Fiona turned the photo over. On the back of the folder, in ink, someone had written *Evelyn and Margaret, 1913.*

Evelyn. And Margaret.

Fiona's brain whirred through memories and names and years.

These two were sisters. Just as obviously as she and Arden were sisters. Evelyn and Margaret had lived in this place, back when it had been a grand old mansion, not a library. Then, many years later, Margaret had died, leaving her house to the town and her portrait hanging above its staircase, overseeing it all.

Evelyn and Margaret *Chisholm*.

Fiona set the photo back on the dresser. Her fingers felt numb. So did her legs. Maybe she was thinking so hard that her body had sent all its blood to her brain, leaving everything else to turn to rubber. She let her gaze drift along the wall until her eyes snagged on something else.

Beside the dresser hung a painting of a vase of roses. And just past the corner of its gilded frame, drilled into the wall, was a small, round hole.

Fiona bent closer.

Through the hole, dimly lit by daylight, was an empty room. But once there had been another girl's bedroom there. And there had been another girl in it. A girl who might have put her face to the hole and whispered—

"What are you doing in here?"

Fiona jumped back.

A woman stood in the bedroom doorway. She was tall and broad, wearing a long black dress and a stern expression. Fiona didn't recognize her, but from the authoritative way she moved and spoke, it was clear that she worked here. Maybe she had an office behind one of the nearest closed doors.

"No one is supposed to use this room," said the woman.

"Sorry," said Fiona, tottering forward on rubbery legs. "I was just following that dog. . . ."

The woman eyed the open closet, where the dog was still huffing at the hanging clothes. "Yes, that *dog*," she said dryly. She snapped her fingers. "Come here, troublemaker."

The dog trotted reluctantly to her side.

"This room is to remain closed," the woman said as Fiona scurried out into the hall. "Undisturbed. Do you understand?"

"Yes." Fiona backed away. "I just . . . sorry."

The woman gave a brusque nod. She stood protectively before the bedroom door, the curly brown dog beside her, as Fiona hurried off.

Fiona started down the steps. The old wood creaked beneath her. The creaks were too loud for her to be sure, but she thought she heard the woman's distant voice say, "Come along, Pixie."

Pixie.

Fiona almost tripped down the rest of the staircase. She grabbed the railing.

Pixie? No. No way. She must have misheard.

Heart thundering in her ribs, Fiona inched back up the staircase.

The upper hallway was deserted.

The woman and the dog might never have been there at all.

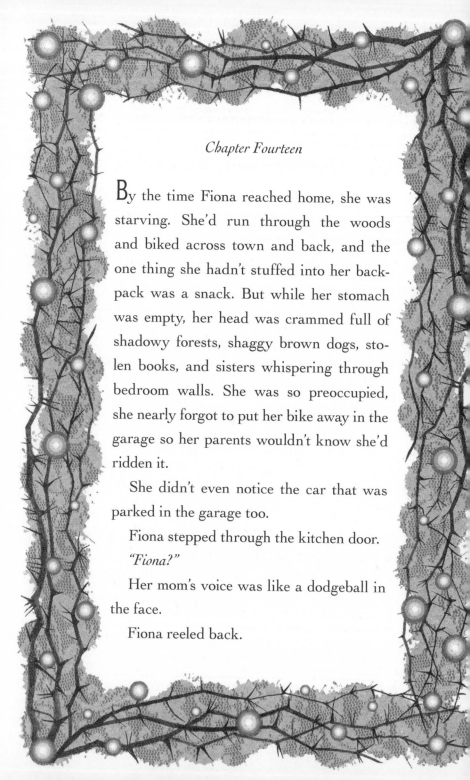

Chapter Fourteen

By the time Fiona reached home, she was starving. She'd run through the woods and biked across town and back, and the one thing she hadn't stuffed into her backpack was a snack. But while her stomach was empty, her head was crammed full of shadowy forests, shaggy brown dogs, stolen books, and sisters whispering through bedroom walls. She was so preoccupied, she nearly forgot to put her bike away in the garage so her parents wouldn't know she'd ridden it.

She didn't even notice the car that was parked in the garage too.

Fiona stepped through the kitchen door. *"Fiona?"*

Her mom's voice was like a dodgeball in the face.

Fiona reeled back.

Caitlin Murphy-Crane strode into the kitchen, cell phone in one hand, receiver of the landline in the other. "Where have you been?"

Fiona's thoughts blew apart. All that remained were several of her own questions, like: what time was it? How had her mom beaten her home? What could Fiona say that *wouldn't* result in very bad things?

"Um . . . ," Fiona stalled. "I rode my bike to the library."

"To the library? When you were told not to leave the house?" The fuzzy elephants dangling from her mom's earlobes jiggled with her words. "You went without leaving a note, and you didn't even answer your phone when I called over and over?"

"My phone?" Fiona reached into her backpack pocket. Three texts. Six missed calls. "Oh. I must have had it on silent."

"I can't believe you would do this. I was so worried, I got out of work early and rushed home. And you just—hold on, your dad is calling me back. Steven?" she said into the cell phone. "No, she's here now. She just came in. Yes, she's all right. . . . the library. I know."

Fiona sidled toward the staircase. Her mom raised a hand, halting her.

"We can talk more when you get home," she continued into the phone. "Yes. How's Arden doing? Really?"

Her face softened slightly, happiness touching it like a thin ray of sun. "That's great."

Fiona felt a spear of resentment. She couldn't even get through a scolding without Arden stealing the spotlight.

"I'm so sorry we couldn't all be there. Yes. Sorry to have made you panic too. See you later." Her mom tapped the screen, her eyes slicing back to Fiona.

"Can you imagine what it feels like to come home and find your child *gone*, without a trace?" She didn't wait for an answer, which was fine, because Fiona didn't have one. "It's lucky I hadn't already called 911."

Her mom finally set down both phones and rubbed her forehead with her fingers. "All right. We'll talk specifics when your dad gets home. But I can promise that you will not be leaving this house for *several* days. You will lose your phone privileges. And it will be a long time before we trust you to go anywhere on your own."

Taking the cell phone out of Fiona's hand, her mom turned and strode toward the staircase.

Fiona rushed after her. "Mom . . . I'm really sorry. I should have left a note. And the phone thing was an accident, I swear."

"Really?" said her mom, reaching the creaky upper hall. "This wasn't your revenge for having to miss Cy's birthday?"

"No," said Fiona, after a telltale pause. "I mean, I was really disappointed. But—"

"That makes two of us," her mom interrupted.

She opened Fiona's bedroom door and lifted the laptop from the desk.

"Computer too?" Fiona gasped. No contact with friends. No Kon-Struct. No way to research any of the names or dates or places that were whirling around the borders of her brain like enraged wasps. "Mom, please—can I just keep the laptop? I need it for research. *Please.*"

"You think you should only get punishments you want?" Her mom shook her head. Her face was sad, like something empty that should have been full.

It reminded Fiona of the dresses dangling in that musty closet.

She needed to learn more about that bedroom. *Evelyn's* bedroom. And her mom was taking away every tool she had.

"I *said* I was sorry." Fiona's voice came out too hard. Too angry.

Her mom looked down at her with those hollow eyes. "I heard you. And I'm glad you're all right. But that's all I'm glad about right now."

Holding Fiona's things, she stepped out the bedroom door, closing it soundly between them.

Fiona stood still, the wasps buzzing out of her brain and down through every vein in her body. Her mom's words weren't even true. That wasn't *all* she was glad about. She was glad about Arden doing well at her competition.

Perfect Arden.

Fiona threw herself down on the bed. An instant later, she bounced up again.

Cautiously, she inched open her bedroom door. The thumps and clunks of her mother moving around the kitchen drifted up from below. Fiona slipped out into the hallway. Keeping close to the wall, where the floorboards were less loose and creaky, she tiptoed to Arden's room.

The door was shut, but not latched. Fiona darted inside. There was still no trace of *The Lost One*, but her sister's tablet lay on the desktop, between a mug of perfectly sharpened pencils and a stack of sparkly notebooks. Fiona snatched it up. With the tablet pinned under her arm, she scuttled back to her own room.

Arden's background image was a picture of French skater Surya Bonaly in the middle of a backflip. Fiona rolled her eyes. Of course it was. But at least Arden hadn't broken the family rule about setting up a lock code.

Fiona hunched over the tablet and got to work.

She began by searching for "Evelyn Chisholm." She wasn't sure what she hoped to find. But if Evelyn and Margaret Chisholm had even more in common with Hazel and Pearl than matching bedrooms in a matching town, there would have to be *some* information about them—something to link them irrefutably with the girls in the book.

She found an old British lady named Evelyn Chisholm, and a few Evelyn Chisholms scattered through the US, but no one from the right era. And nothing about a girl who disappeared.

She tried "Margaret Chisholm" next. There were a million listings, all of them about the Margaret Chisholm Memorial Library. That was a dead end.

Fiona tried "Lost Lake disappearance" and "Lost Lake Searcher," which turned up nothing but newspaper stories about a missing pet cat.

Fiona's eyes were beginning to sting. And she was running out of time. Her dad and her sister could be home at any minute.

"Evelyn." Fiona tried again. But this time she was typing so fast that she hit enter without adding anything more.

Evelyn. Evelyn. Evelyn. A long list of baby name sites popped up. Fiona was about to start over when a word halfway down the screen halted her.

Evelyn, read one entry. *From the Norman French "Aveline," meaning hazelnut.*

The back of Fiona's neck prickled.

Hazel.

With shaky hands, she typed "Margaret" and hit enter.

Margaret, read the very first line on the page. *From the old Persian word for pearl.*

Pearl.

The threads braided themselves together so fast that Fiona's mind spun.

Hazel and Pearl from *The Lost One* and Evelyn and Margaret Chisholm from Lost Lake weren't just similar. They were the same. They had lived in the same house—the house that was now the Lost Lake library. They had played in the same woods. And one of them had vanished in the very same way.

Whoever had written *The Lost One* must have known the whole story. But they'd written only half of it down, changing enough details to make a reader dig for the truth.

But *why?* Fiona pummeled her brain with the question. Why tell only part of the story? Did whoever had written it expect—or hope—that some reader would finally figure it out?

A downstairs door slammed. Voices echoed through the house.

Switching the tablet off, Fiona scrambled back along the hall and left it neatly aligned on Arden's desk. She flew back to her own bedroom.

Everything that would happen next—more lecturing from her parents, a family dinner that was taken up entirely by talk about Arden and her competition, being sent off to bed early—didn't matter.

Fiona had found something. Something huge. Something world-changing. She felt like Howard Carter peering through the door of King Tutankhamun's tomb.

She was on the threshold. And inside, there was more to find.

Chapter Fifteen

Fiona was grounded for the entire week.

On Monday morning, her parents headed off to work, leaving Arden and Fiona in the house together. Arden stayed so icily silent, Fiona might as well have been there alone. Fiona knew there was no point asking Arden what she'd done with *The Lost One*. Her sister would only lie, if she spoke to her at all.

They finished their breakfast in stifling quiet. Arden cleared her dishes and stalked into the living room.

"I'll be upstairs!" Fiona shouted after her.

Arden didn't answer.

That was fine with Fiona. Her words weren't a peace offering. They were an alibi.

Shut in her bedroom, Fiona pulled the curtains and switched off the lights, making everything as dim as possible. She wadded a pile of dirty laundry under the bedspread, so

if Arden happened to glance in—which wasn't likely—
she'd think Fiona was curled up in bed, taking a sulky
nap. Then Fiona waited.

At last, when she heard her sister's footsteps on
the stairs, followed by the closing bathroom door and
the pipe-creaking hiss of the shower, Fiona took her
chance.

She slung her backpack over her shoulder, bolted out
of the house, and biked away as fast as she could ride.

A funny feeling struck her as she climbed the steps
of Chisholm Memorial Library.

These were the steps that Pearl had bounded up
while being chased by the Searcher. This was the doorway where Pixie had waited, keeping guard. This was
Pearl and Hazel's house.

No—*Margaret and Evelyn's* house. When Fiona
stepped across the threshold, she felt like both a guest
and a trespasser, like she was stepping into the past and
the present at the very same time.

The librarian with the bow tie—it was a purple one
this morning—smiled at her as she slipped by. "Can I
help you find anything today?"

"No, thank you, Mr. Owens," said Fiona.

Today she wasn't looking for a book.

She was looking for that blond-haired boy.

She knew he lived on Church Street, but she didn't

know his house number, or even his name. Her only real option was searching where she'd found him in the first place.

Fiona had just finished checking the upstairs rooms and was padding back along the walkway when, in the central chamber below her, a familiar figure caught her eye.

It wasn't the blond boy.

Someone with swirly brown hair topped by a little bouquet of violets had just emerged from the research room.

Fiona watched as Ms. Miranda glanced carefully around the room, making sure that Mr. Owens was busy helping a patron at the computers before ducking behind the circulation desk. Once more, the librarian glanced to either side. But she didn't look up.

From above, Fiona watched as Ms. Miranda crouched behind the desk. The librarian pulled something dark green and book-shaped from under her arm, stuffed it into a canvas shoulder bag, and hid the bag behind a wastebasket. Then, with one last look around, she rose and strode away, leaving the desk unoccupied.

Fiona sucked in a gasp that felt full of static electricity. Her book—*The Lost One*—was *here.*

But how? And why? And did it even matter? Did

anything matter more than getting that book back in her own hands?

Fiona flew down the staircase. Mr. Owens was still busy at the computers. No one else was watching as she dove behind the circulation desk. She landed on her hands and knees, yanking the canvas bag out from behind the wastebasket.

The Lost One was waiting for her inside. Its soft cover fit into her grasp like a familiar hand.

Clutching the book to her chest, Fiona whirled around—straight into someone's pink silk shirt.

"Whoa," said Ms. Miranda, taking an off-balance step back. "Well, hi there, Fiona Crane." Her clear brown eyes flicked to the book in Fiona's arms. "I guess the two of us need to have a chat."

The storage room down the STAFF ONLY hallway was tile floored and dim. One glance around reminded Fiona that this had once been the kitchen. Wooden cabinets still lined its walls, and the faintest scent of cinnamon and cloves haunted the air.

"We can talk in here," said Ms. Miranda, flipping on a light. She stepped past Fiona toward the middle of the room.

Fiona hung back in the doorway. She gripped *The Lost One* tight, trying to crush a hundred questions into the back of her mind, where they couldn't flood out all at once and give her secrets away.

Ms. Miranda perched on a heavy table, facing Fiona. The bouquet of violets in her hair nodded softly. She reached into the pocket of her shirt.

Fiona's first thought was that Ms. Miranda was pulling out a gun.

But that was ridiculous. A librarian would choose a quieter weapon. Something like poison, or a nice tight gag.

Fiona stepped backward. Her spine struck the door.

Ms. Miranda took a cardboard package from her pocket. "Chocolate-covered raisins?"

Fiona blinked. "What?"

"Chocolate always helps me think." The librarian leaned forward, holding out the box. "Want some?"

Cautiously, Fiona stepped closer, one hand out. Ms. Miranda poured several chocolates into it before eating one herself. So the raisins *couldn't* be poisoned, Fiona thought. That seemed like a good sign.

"Okay," Ms. Miranda began. "You've read the library's strangest book. What did you think?"

"It was . . . interesting," Fiona answered carefully. "Except for the missing ending."

"Annoying, isn't it?" said Ms. Miranda. "It might be the worst misprint I've ever seen. Except you can't really have a *misprint* if a book was never printed."

"Never printed?" Fiona echoed.

"I've done the research. There's no record of *The Lost One* ever being published." Ms. Miranda pointed at the book in Fiona's arms. "That's the only copy that has ever existed. And it's incomplete. See? *Annoying.*"

"Wait," said Fiona, feeling like time was suddenly reeling backward. "You know all about the book. But you told me the library didn't even have it." She gripped the book harder. "Why did you lie?"

"I didn't lie. Honest." Ms. Miranda gave a small smile. "That book is not part of our fiction collection. No one is supposed to check it out. Or even know about it, really."

Fiona frowned. "Then . . . why is it here?"

"It belongs upstairs, in the private rooms. It's one of the Chisholms' personal possessions. They're supposed to stay undisturbed."

"But someone disturbed them anyway," Fiona pointed out. "Because I found this on the shelves in the mystery room."

"Really?" Ms. Miranda tipped her head to one side. The violets tipped too. "You weren't possibly poking around in staff-only areas . . . ?"

"No!" said Fiona. "Well . . . I mean—not *then.* It was in the mystery room. I swear."

Ms. Miranda ate another chocolate. "Okay. Maybe it was."

"Which means someone *else* moved it," Fiona pushed on.

"Maybe." Ms. Miranda shook a few more chocolates out of the box. "That book is *supposed* to stay on the third floor, like I said. But it has a habit of traveling all over the library. It will turn up in one of the reading rooms, or on top of a shelf somewhere. Today I found it under a chair in the research room." She shrugged, shaking her head. "I always return it to the third floor, where it belongs, and eventually it pops up somewhere else." Her bright eyes met Fiona's. "My guess is you're not the only library visitor who likes to wander through our off-limits areas."

"So is that how the book got back to the library now?" Fiona asked. "Did you steal it from my house?"

"From your *house*?" Ms. Miranda looked at her dubiously. "No. I've never stolen a book from a reader's house, no matter how overdue or off-limits it was." She gave a little grin. "If you smuggled that book out, and it ended up back here somehow . . ." The grin faded slightly. "I'm honestly not sure what to say."

"But . . ." Fiona shook her head. The hundreds of questions inside sloshed around. "Wait. Why didn't you tell me all this about *The Lost One* back when I asked?"

One of Ms. Miranda's eyebrows rose. "Well, first, if you had found that book, it was fairly likely that you'd been snooping in off-limits parts of the library. That didn't make you seem one hundred percent trustworthy. Second, if I'd told you that the book you're holding is a one-of-a-kind, unfinished mystery that's not supposed to leave its bedroom, wouldn't I basically have been *telling* you to steal it?"

Fiona chewed a chocolate, stalling. "I guess I *might* have tried to take it," she answered. "Probably."

"And third . . ." Ms. Miranda's eyes flickered over Fiona's face, and Fiona had the sensation that she was being read like fine print on a page. "You know what? Why don't you tell me what you've figured out about the story first?"

Fiona swallowed.

How far could she trust Ms. Miranda? And did it even matter, when she was already caught, trapped in a dead end of unfinished stories?

"I know the story is set here, in Lost Lake," she began slowly. "I know Hazel and Pearl were really Evelyn and Margaret Chisholm. I know they lived here, in this house."

"Very good," said Ms. Miranda. In her eyes, which were still focused on Fiona's face, there wasn't a single glimmer of surprise. "You're right. Hazel and Pearl were obviously inspired by Evelyn and Margaret Chisholm."

"That's why I need to find out the ending," said Fiona, speaking faster now. "I know about the Searcher, and how Evelyn disappeared—but I need to know what really happened. Because if the place and the people are all real, then the story must be *true*."

Ms. Miranda kept quiet for a beat. "I used to have that theory too," she said at last. Her voice was gentler than before. "After I read the story for the first time— the part of the story that exists, anyway—I looked into it. But the problem is: it *isn't* true." Ms. Miranda's words came out softly, slowly, clearly. "Evelyn Chisholm didn't disappear at all. She died."

Fiona rocked back. "You mean—did somebody—"

"It was nothing criminal," Ms. Miranda stopped her. "She got sick. Probably pneumonia. She passed away in her own bed, right upstairs."

A shiver ran from Fiona's feet to the top of her spine. No wonder there had been a strange hush in that room. "But . . ." She shook her head again, trying to pull these new ideas together. "But if Evelyn just *died*, and everyone knew where and how, then why would someone turn it into a mystery? Why would somebody make up just *half* of a story?"

"That's what people do," said Ms. Miranda simply. "When they don't know a whole story, they make one up." She leaned back on the table. "I've lived and worked here for six years now. I know a few things about local history, including the kinds of things that don't always get written down. Like that there were rumors about the Chisholm family long before Evelyn died."

"Rumors?"

"This is a small town," said Ms. Miranda. "And the Chisholms didn't quite fit into it. They moved here, instead of coming from here. They were rich. They were a little odd. And Margaret and Evelyn were the oddest, running around in the woods all day, getting into all kinds of trouble. It's not what people expected little rich girls to do back then. So the rest of the town spread stories about them. Some of them are *still* going around. Like that Evelyn ran off with the circus. Or she was snatched by the Searcher. Or that she was killed by someone in her own household, and they all covered it up."

These words seemed to dangle in the air for a moment.

Fiona suddenly felt the entire house looming around them, as though it were listening in. It would be very easy to concoct creepy stories about a house like this.

"That's . . ." She trailed off, searching for the right conclusion.

"That's Lost Lake." Ms. Miranda shrugged. "That's any old, small town. When I moved here for this job, there were all kinds of whispers about *me*."

"Really?"

"Oh, sure. I wasn't *from here*. I was from *Philly*, which made me very suspicious." Ms. Miranda grinned. "There was gossip about the programs I ran, the books I bought. There was gossip about my personal life. There was even gossip about the way I dressed. Finally I started putting one weird thing in my hair every day, just so they'd have something good to whisper about." She touched the violets above her ear, grinning wider. "Maybe you've noticed it too, being new here. Lost Lake isn't the friendliest place to anybody who doesn't already belong."

The words loosened a little of the tightness that had been crushing Fiona's ribs ever since their move. "Yeah," she answered, taking a deep breath. "I have noticed that."

"That's the main reason I'm protective of that book." Ms. Miranda nodded at *The Lost One*. "This town doesn't need any more material for gossip about the Chisholms. They deserve to be left in peace."

Fiona cradled the book closer. "If the whole town spread stories about the family, then who wrote this one?"

Long Lost

"Who knows?" said Ms. Miranda. "Anyone who knew the Chisholms could have done it. And they would have had good reasons to stay anonymous."

Something else tickled the back of Fiona's mind.

"Are you *positive* about how Evelyn died?" she asked carefully. "Like . . . are there any official records or documents, or . . ."

Ms. Miranda broke into another grin. "Are you sure you don't want to become a librarian?" She slid down from the table and crossed toward a shelf stuffed with filing boxes. "Documents. I *love* documents." She pulled a flat cardboard box from the highest shelf. "Here we are."

She extended two pages toward Fiona.

Fiona wiped the traces of chocolate from her palm onto her jeans, set *The Lost One* carefully on the counter, and took them.

The topmost sheet was a photocopied newspaper clipping.

The Lost Lake Herald, June 1913

Evelyn Rose Chisholm, eldest daughter of prominent local resident Frederick Chisholm, has passed away peacefully after a brief illness at the age of thirteen years. She is survived by her parents, Frederick and Clara Chisholm, and her beloved sister Margaret. She will be dearly missed by all who knew her. *Private funeral services were held at Emmanuel Episcopal Church. Interment was in Wayfarer's Rest Cemetery in Lost Lake.*

Fiona turned to the second paper.

It was a letter. A letter typed on an old typewriter, the kind that pressed tiny dents into the page.

May 4, 1970

To whom it may concern,

As has been arranged by my attorneys, I am leaving my family home to Lost Lake, to house its public library. I'm pleased to know that this place will remain a living part of the town even when I, the last of the Chisholms of Lost Lake, am gone.

Before considering the arrangement final, I make one request that I trust the library will honor.

While renovations and updates may prove necessary, I ask that the bedroom of my elder sister, Evelyn, be left intact and untouched in perpetuity. Evelyn's room has been kept just as she left it when she passed away in 1913. Perhaps preserving her room allowed those of us who knew her to maintain the hope that Evelyn would one day come back. Perhaps we simply could not bear to do otherwise.

Copies of this letter have been provided to both the library board and my attorneys. I expect my requests to be reflected in all future contracts pertaining to the property.

There was a signature beneath the last typed line: *Margaret A. Chisholm.*

Fiona rubbed the edges of the page with her fingertips. Nothing felt quite as real as a typed, signed document.

"It's always more satisfying to see evidence firsthand, isn't it?" said Ms. Miranda. She took the papers back, placing them gently into their box. "Even if it doesn't tell you what you expected it to."

"What about the Searcher?" Fiona raced after a last loose thread. "You don't think *that* could have been real, do you? I mean . . . if everybody in town believed in it—"

"The Searcher is just another story." Ms. Miranda slid the box onto its shelf. "There are no weird beings wandering around in the woods, grabbing people. There's no Searcher."

"But if lots of people saw it, like the book says . . . ," Fiona persisted, even though her voice was growing smaller. "I mean, I even thought I might have seen it in the woods the other day. . . ."

"You know that old expression . . . 'Seeing is believing'?" Ms. Miranda asked. She moved slowly back toward Fiona. "It's backward. You've heard a story about something called the Searcher. Then you see something a little strange, maybe just a shadow in the woods, and your mind starts telling you that story. You tell it to other people, and they start seeing things that must be part of the story too. Soon so many people believe in the Searcher, they see it everywhere. That's how stories work."

Ms. Miranda stopped in front of Fiona, giving her a wry but sympathetic little smile. She held out one hand. "Now. Would you like to kick this annoying book around the room for a while before I put it away again?"

The words were joking, but Fiona felt a sudden tightness shoot through her body. She couldn't let go of the book. Not again. Not already.

"Can I . . . could I take it home with me?" she asked. "Just for a little while?"

Ms. Miranda's smile dimmed. "Sorry," she said. "Archival materials aren't supposed to leave the building."

"I just want to check it again." Fiona pulled back. "There has to be something else to learn. *Please.*"

Ms. Miranda's face was kind but firm. "It's just a sad old story, Fiona. It might not have any more to tell you."

"But it *might.* And I just . . . since we moved to Lost Lake, I've felt like there was no reason for me to be here." Fiona's words came faster. "Like I was just getting dragged along by my sister. But maybe I can figure out this mystery. Maybe it's been waiting for the right person to come along. Maybe then I won't feel . . ." Fiona swallowed the words that surged inside her. *So lonely. So unwanted. So forgotten.* "I don't know," she finished. "But maybe this is my reason."

Ms. Miranda gazed down at Fiona for a long moment. "You might be right," she said. "About the story waiting for someone to understand it. Margaret Chisholm certainly deserves that." She put one hand lightly on Fiona's shoulder. "You'll make a great historian someday, you know. Or a great librarian." A fraction of her smile curled back. "Take the book," she murmured. "Just don't tell anyone. Take perfect care of it, and bring it back *soon*. Got it?"

Fiona was already nodding eagerly.

Ms. Miranda nodded too. "I've got to get back to work. Come and see me if you need anything else. Anything except more chocolate-covered raisins, because I just finished them. All right?"

"I will," Fiona promised.

The click of Ms. Miranda's steps trailed out of the storage room.

Fiona stood by herself in the former kitchen, hugging *The Lost One* tight. She combed through the thoughts in her head, trying to separate the facts from the guesses, rereading them like the old documents that Ms. Miranda had handed over.

An idea lanced through her.

There was one more place to look for evidence. Why hadn't she thought of it before?

A moment later, with *The Lost One* zipped safely inside her backpack, Fiona rushed out of the library and onto her bike.

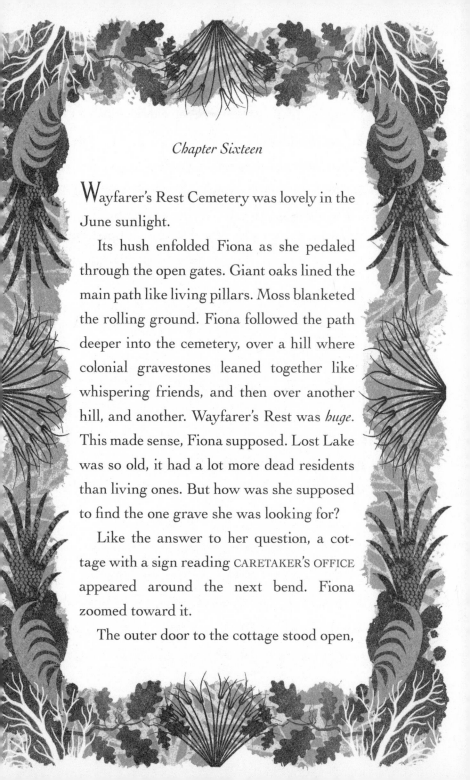

Chapter Sixteen

Wayfarer's Rest Cemetery was lovely in the June sunlight.

Its hush enfolded Fiona as she pedaled through the open gates. Giant oaks lined the main path like living pillars. Moss blanketed the rolling ground. Fiona followed the path deeper into the cemetery, over a hill where colonial gravestones leaned together like whispering friends, and then over another hill, and another. Wayfarer's Rest was *huge*. This made sense, Fiona supposed. Lost Lake was so old, it had a lot more dead residents than living ones. But how was she supposed to find the one grave she was looking for?

Like the answer to her question, a cottage with a sign reading CARETAKER'S OFFICE appeared around the next bend. Fiona zoomed toward it.

The outer door to the cottage stood open,

a flimsy screen door letting in the grassy air. Fiona pushed the latch and stepped inside.

A man with thick glasses and a steaming mug in his hands was just emerging from a nook in the back.

"Morning," he said, giving her a not-too-friendly nod. He obviously knew she didn't belong here, Fiona thought. And not just because she was alive. He crossed the office toward a large metal desk. "Need something?"

"Yes," said Fiona. "I need to find a grave."

"That's why most people come here," said the man, sitting down at the desk. "Name?"

"My name? Fiona Crane."

Now the man looked mildly surprised. "Is the grave for you?"

"Oh. *No,*" said Fiona. "I thought—never mind. I'm looking for the Chisholm family plot."

"Ah. Chisholms." The man leaned back in the chair. "Don't need to check the files for that one. Built themselves the biggest house in town. Guess they needed the biggest monument to go with it." He took a sip of coffee. "It's right over on Silver Birch. By the pond."

"The pond?" Fiona repeated.

With an almost silent sigh, the man pulled a laminated map out of a desk drawer. Fiona bent eagerly over it.

"Here's Oak Lane," he said, tapping a black line.

"That's the road you came in on. Here's Silver Birch, where you'll make a left. If you get to the pond, you've missed it. But you probably won't miss it. The Chisholms wanted to be noticed. At least for some things."

"You mean there were things they *didn't* want noticed?" Fiona asked. "Did you know them?"

"Naw," said the man. "Just heard plenty." He tapped the map again before sliding it back into the drawer. "Left on Silver Birch."

"Okay," said Fiona, sidling back toward the screen door. "Thank you."

She pedaled along the path, turning at the sign for Silver Birch. The branching pavement was narrower here, but the gravestones along it became grander and grander, growing from skull-and-bones headstones to stone mausoleums and towering marble obelisks. And there, on the tallest pillar of all:

CHISHOLM

Fiona dropped her bike onto the moss. She scurried closer, her heart starting to thump.

In front of the obelisk were two large matching headstones.

FREDERICK R. CHISHOLM 1866–1931

CLARA M. CHISHOLM 1867–1928

Fiona looked to both sides, breathing harder.

A few steps to the left, sheltered by two evergreen

bushes, was a newer, smaller, grayer headstone.

Margaret A. Chisholm 1902–1971

Fiona gazed past the gray headstone, into the shadows cast by a thicket of pine trees.

There.

The trees had grown thick enough that the stone between them was easy to miss. Its edges had sunk into the soft earth, and moss and lichen had crept close, covering its corners like green cobwebs.

Fiona crouched beside it.

Evelyn Rose Chisholm

Darling Daughter–

Beloved Sister

Fiona touched the face of the stone, very gently. It was cold and solid and real.

Maybe Ms. Miranda wasn't concealing anything after all. Maybe she was right about the story in *The Lost One* being a lie. Because Evelyn hadn't disappeared at all. She was right here. She'd been here all along.

Fiona sagged down on the damp grass.

She'd been fooling herself. She had wanted so badly to find something meaningful to do in Lost Lake that she had clung to this silly quest—just like she had when she was a bored little kid waiting at Arden's skating rink, pretending that the bits of trash she found in the stands were relics of an ancient civilization.

There was nothing here to discover. Nothing that needed Fiona to find it.

Feeling suddenly fifty pounds heavier, she hauled herself back onto her bike.

In the oily dimness of her family's garage, with the book still zipped securely in her bag, Fiona stopped to think.

Arden might have noticed she was missing by now. But she didn't have *proof* that Fiona had left the house. If Fiona was careful, she might be able to get back up to her bedroom without Arden spotting her.

She inched open the garage door.

Arden was sitting at the kitchen table.

A notepad and a set of neatly sharpened colored pencils lay beside her. She was wearing earbuds, but she tugged them out as Fiona stepped inside. She didn't speak. A tiny lift of her eyebrows told Fiona that Arden had been waiting for her.

Fiona felt the air whoosh out of her body.

"How long have you been sitting there?"

"Right here?" Arden tapped the table with the end of a pale blue pencil. "Not that long. I've just been working on my planner, listening to my program music. But I noticed you were gone *forever* ago." One corner of her mouth started to smile. "Making a fake body in the bed?

Seriously? When has that ever worked, outside of the movies?"

"I just had to get something from the library," said Fiona tightly. "It was urgent."

"Um-hmm," said Arden, in a way that might have meant she believed this or not, and that it didn't matter either way.

"I suppose you're going to tell on me?" Fiona clenched both fists. "Ruin my life even more?"

The smile on Arden's lips disappeared. "I wasn't *going* to. Even if I probably should."

Fiona tried to read her sister's face, but over the past couple of years, Arden's face had gotten very hard to read. Much harder than the fine print in an old book. "You *weren't* going to tell?"

"I didn't tell that you trashed my room the other day," said Arden coolly. "Even though I know it was you."

"I thought you had taken a book of mine without asking."

Arden flashed Fiona a baffled look. "I'd probably borrow your *toothbrush* before I borrowed one of your weird books." She set the pencil down. "Listen. We're old enough to handle some problems ourselves, right?"

"Right," said Fiona uncertainly.

"So, we can do that now. If we agree on a few things."

"Like what?" Dread began to crystalize in Fiona's stomach. "Are you going to force me to do your laundry and dust your trophies and come clap at all your practices or something?"

"No," said Arden. "I know you'd never come clap for me anyway."

The words were so bitter, Fiona took a teeny step backward.

Arden rolled the pencil back and forth under her fingers. "I know something is going on with you," she said. "You've got some new project or obsession that you're working on, and it obviously has to do with the library, or research, or whatever. And by the way, sneaking out of the house when you're grounded just to go to the *library* is the most Fiona-ish thing you could possibly do."

Fiona almost smiled. But she wouldn't have wanted Arden to see it.

"And maybe I feel kind of bad," Arden went on. "About you having to leave your friends and missing that party and everything. So I'm going to be *extra* understanding. And in exchange, you can do something for me."

"Like what?" said Fiona.

"I don't know yet. I'll decide when the time comes. For now, we'll just say that you owe me a big favor, and when I ask you for it, you won't say no."

Fiona thought. Arden could demand something really unpleasant. Something that could cause serious trouble. But what options did she have? It was say yes and maybe hurt herself in the future, or say no and definitely hurt herself now.

"Fine," she answered.

"Good." Arden tapped the pencil on the tabletop again. *Tap tap tap.*

Fiona squared her shoulders. If Arden was waiting for her to explain, or to apologize, or to even *start* making up, she was going to be disappointed.

"I'm going to my room," she said at last, grasping both backpack straps and heading toward the hall.

But Arden was already fitting her earbuds back into place.

Upstairs, Fiona flopped across her bed. She unzipped her backpack and pulled out *The Lost One*. She flipped through the pages to the point where the story broke off, as though somehow this time things would be different. It wasn't.

She was flipping through the blank pages so quickly that all she saw at first was one flash of paler white. Fiona stopped and turned slowly backward.

Someone had wedged a scrap of notebook paper between the blank pages. And written on it, in blocky, tilted letters, was a message.

Don't stop now. You're on the right track. KEEP DIGGING.

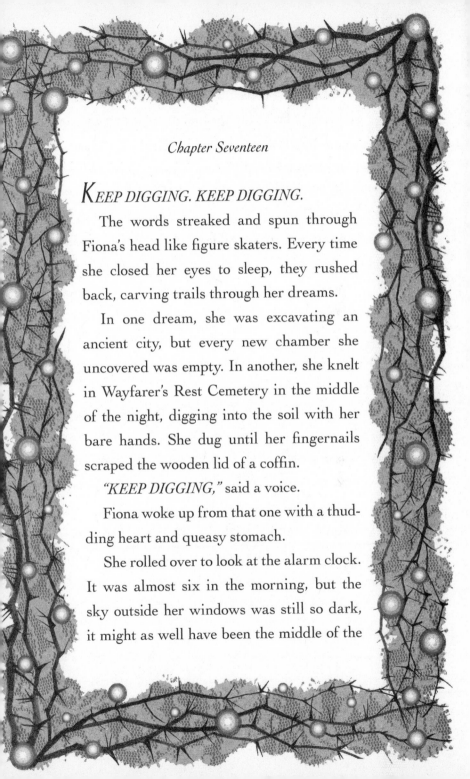

Chapter Seventeen

KEEP DIGGING. KEEP DIGGING.

The words streaked and spun through Fiona's head like figure skaters. Every time she closed her eyes to sleep, they rushed back, carving trails through her dreams.

In one dream, she was excavating an ancient city, but every new chamber she uncovered was empty. In another, she knelt in Wayfarer's Rest Cemetery in the middle of the night, digging into the soil with her bare hands. She dug until her fingernails scraped the wooden lid of a coffin.

"KEEP DIGGING," said a voice.

Fiona woke up from that one with a thudding heart and queasy stomach.

She rolled over to look at the alarm clock. It was almost six in the morning, but the sky outside her windows was still so dark, it might as well have been the middle of the night. Below the occasional booms of thunder, she could hear her family hurrying around, showering, making coffee, rushing off to another day. The house creaked and groaned like it had been awakened too early and wanted to get back to sleep.

Fiona shoved a hand under her pillows and felt the worn leather cover of *The Lost One*. Then she flipped the pillows over, just to make sure. Yes, the book was right where she'd left it. And the note on the scrap of paper was there too.

KEEP DIGGING.

Who had left the note? And why? And what did it mean?

Fiona tried to think logically, even though logic barely seemed to matter anymore.

Who had access to the book? Well . . . Ms. Miranda, of course. Was she trying to send Fiona a secret message, something that she couldn't say aloud? Or was it the weird blond boy, who clearly knew something about the story? Was it the woman who worked on the library's third floor, and who obviously cared about protecting Evelyn's memory? Could it be someone else? Could it be a *trick*?

Fiona put the pillow back over the book. Then she flopped down and thumped her head against the pillows, which sometimes helped to shake thoughts loose.

If the book didn't have any more answers to give, where could she look? She'd checked the graveyard. She'd explored the woods around Parson's Bridge and hadn't found anything but a stray dog—a dog who'd led her straight back to the library. The library that was Evelyn and Margaret's house.

That had to be it. There had to be something there for Fiona to find. Something that would prove the story in *The Lost One* was true after all.

Suddenly, Fiona sat straight up in bed. *KEEP DIGGING.*

She knew just what she needed to look for.

The stormy sky was darkening from pencil lead to charcoal when Fiona pedaled up to the old brick mansion.

She had waited until her family left the house before tucking *The Lost One* into her bed, putting on a raincoat, and sneaking into the garage. Then she'd zipped a garden trowel into her backpack and steered her bike out into the rain.

It was just past seven now, nearly two hours before the library would open. The rest of downtown Lost Lake was dim and sleepy, doors shut and windows dark. Still, Fiona felt the quiet old buildings watching her, as if they knew she shouldn't have been there at all.

At the library, Fiona turned, riding around the big

brick building and into the backyard. There she stopped and scanned the windows. There were no lights on yet. No one was inside to look out and see her creeping past.

Fiona examined the wooded yard. The sagging building to her left had to be the old carriage house. Fiona imagined Charlie Hobbes peering out of its boarded-up second-floor windows, watching a girl in a white nightgown trail into the trees.

But which tree had she chosen?

Thunder rumbled, closer now. Fiona blinked the raindrops from her eyelashes. There were dozens of oaks to pick from. Which one was the biggest? Which was the oldest? How could she possibly know? She thought of archeologists surveying miles of blank, bare desert, deciding where to dig. How could *they* possibly know?

At least archeologists had teams, she thought, pulling the trowel out of her backpack. They didn't have to search all alone.

But when she straightened up again, Fiona wasn't alone either.

Something hidden in the trees was watching her with yellow eyes.

Fiona's heart jolted.

She took two quick steps back, skidding on the slippery grass.

The yellow eyes stared on.

They were too close to the ground to be human. Fiona was pretty sure that there weren't any dangerous wild animals in this part of Massachusetts, but when the eyes suddenly charged closer, Fiona's heart jolted again.

Before she could run, a curly brown dog bounded out of the shadows.

"Oh. It's *you*." The words came out of her in a relieved whoosh. "What are you doing out in the rain?"

She stepped toward the dog, but just like before, it danced out of her reach.

"Hey. Dog!" Fiona called. "Where do you live?"

The dog circled a nearby tree, sniffing at something on the ground.

"Are you a stray? Or do you belong here?"

The dog pawed at the earth.

Fiona lowered her voice and tried once more. "Hey. Is your name *Pixie*?"

At this, the dog looked up. Its gold-brown eyes met hers. Its bristly nose quivered.

Fiona stood like a stone, letting the rain pummel her.

It couldn't be. It couldn't be the *same* Pixie. The same curly brown dog that had lived here, with Evelyn and Margaret, more than a hundred years ago.

Fiona crouched. "Come here, Pixie," she whispered.

Now the dog padded closer. But when Fiona reached out to touch him, she felt nothing but a stir in the cold, damp air.

A matching cold, damp feeling swirled through Fiona's stomach.

The dog turned away again, pawing harder at the roots of the tree.

Like he was looking for something.

In Fiona's head, a match touched a wick. She grabbed the trowel.

The dog hopped sideways, watching, as Fiona began to dig.

The ground was spongy with rain. As Fiona dug, the drops fell faster, the hole around her trowel pooling with rainwater. Soon the dirt turned to mud. Cold grit stuck between her fingers, and wet strands of hair pasted themselves to her face.

The dog gave an impatient whimper.

Flickers of lightning bleached the air. Thunder banged again, so close now that it made Fiona jump.

This was ridiculous. What was she doing, crouching under a giant tree during a thunderstorm, gripping a metal tool, taking direction from a dog? Fiona's shoulders sagged. She yanked the trowel out of the mud.

And below it, deep in the muddy hole, something glinted.

Fiona shoved the trowel beneath the glinting thing. It popped to the surface. Fiona grabbed it, letting the pouring rain help wash the mud away.

Underneath was the gleam of mother-of-pearl.

It was coated with dirt and rust, but that didn't matter. Fiona knew what this was.

She was holding Hazel's—*Evelyn's*—pocketknife.

"I knew it," said a voice from behind her.

There was another bang of thunder.

Fiona scrambled around, nearly falling on her backside. Standing a few feet away, holding a broad green umbrella, was the round-faced blond boy.

He nodded toward the knife in Fiona's hand. "I knew it still had to be here somewhere." He squinted through the rain. "How did you know where to look?"

"I . . . ," Fiona began. "The dog was . . ."

She pointed. But the curly brown dog had vanished.

"Oh, you mean Pixie," said the boy.

Fiona swallowed. "You know about Pixie?"

"Sure," said the boy. "Of course I know about him." He gave Fiona a steady stare. "I'm Charlie Hobbes."

Chapter Eighteen

The wet world around Fiona seemed to tilt sideways.

"Charlie Hobbes," she whispered. "The one who buried the knife here in the first place."

"Well, not *that* Charlie Hobbes," said the boy, like Fiona had just declared that one plus one equals eleven. "I'm obviously not a hundred and twenty years old. *That* Charlie Hobbes was my great-grandpa."

"Oh." Fiona let out a tight breath. Cautiously, she reached out with the tip of the trowel and tapped the boy on the arm. It left a streak of mud on his sleeve.

"I'm alive," he said calmly. "But that dog isn't. I mean, not anymore."

"But I saw . . . ," Fiona began. She stopped there. Her arms felt suddenly very heavy, and she couldn't quite remember how to move them.

"I know," said the boy. He glanced up at the rumbling sky. "We should talk somewhere else. Come on. I know where we can go."

He walked away quickly. Fiona couldn't think of anything to do except grab her bag and stumble after him.

The Perch Diner had white beadboard walls and linoleum floors. Rows of blue booths ran along each side, and a counter covered with pie stands stood in between. The scents of coffee, bacon, and cinnamon grabbed Fiona by the nose as she followed Charlie Hobbes through the door.

The Perch Diner. She'd heard that name somewhere before.

"I have a coupon for free oatmeal here," Fiona said aloud.

Charlie Hobbes was folding up his umbrella. He gave her a slightly puzzled look. "I don't really like oatmeal."

"Yeah," said Fiona awkwardly. "Me neither."

Charlie led the way to a booth. There were several other people in the diner, all of them much older, scattered around in singles or pairs. They gave Charlie little nods as he passed by. Then their eyes moved to Fiona, and she could feel them evaluating her, trying to place her, realizing that she didn't belong.

Their murmurs followed her across the room.

". . . into the Putnams' old place, down on Lane's End," she heard one old man say. "One daughter's a big-time skater. Thinks she's going to get to the Olympics or something."

There was a laugh—not a nice one—in response. Fiona had to fight to keep from turning back and snapping that Arden *was* going to get to the Olympics. These people had learned the facts about her family somehow. But then they had twisted them all around.

Charlie sat down in a blue booth. Fiona slid onto the vinyl seat across from him, tugging off the hood of her raincoat. The warm air felt good on her clammy skin. Before she could ask him any questions, or even decide which one to ask first, a large white woman bustled over from behind the counter.

"Hey, sweetie." She plunked down a mug of cocoa in front of Charlie. The tag pinned to her apron read JUDY. "Who's your friend?"

Fiona's brain snagged on the word "friend." Was that what she and this boy were? Friends?

"This is Fiona Crane," Charlie answered. "Her family just moved here. They live down Lane's End Road."

"Ah. So you bought the Putnams' old house," said Judy. Her voice was loud and warm, but her face was hard to read. "Heard they'd sold to a family from western Mass. Welcome to Lost Lake."

"This is my grandma," Charlie told Fiona. "She runs this place."

"Hi," Fiona managed.

"Cocoa for you too?" asked Judy.

"Sure." Fiona halted, reaching into her pocket. "But I don't have any—"

Judy was already striding away.

"Don't worry. You won't have to pay for it." Charlie leaned forward. "The knife," he said, in a lower voice. "Can we look at it?"

After making sure none of the nearby people were watching, Fiona dug the dirty lump out of her raincoat pocket. Charlie made a mat of paper napkins on the tabletop. Fiona set the lump down, and they both craned over it, rubbing it with more napkins until the mud was gone and the mother-of-pearl handle glinted softly in the light.

"Yep. That is definitely Evelyn's knife," said Charlie.

Fiona stared into his face. "You're the one who left me the note, aren't you?" she asked. "You told me to keep digging."

"I knew you were trying to figure out what really happened, just like me," he answered. "I saw you with the book. I heard you asking questions. I thought maybe we could help each other."

"*The Lost One*?" Fiona whispered. "You've read it too?"

"A few weeks ago," Charlie answered. "I've read part of every section in the library, and *all* of some sections. I found it when I was looking through the geology books. At first I pulled it out because I knew it didn't belong there. Then I read a little of it, and I realized it was about Lost Lake and the girls in the story had to be the Chisholms. I tried to check it out, but Ms. Miranda wouldn't let me, because she said it wasn't supposed to circulate at all. So then I snuck it home with me. But it disappeared. Right off the desk in my bedroom." His intent green eyes stared into hers. "Three days later, I found it back at the library again."

"What?" Fiona breathed. "You—"

Abruptly, Charlie sat up, tossing a napkin over the pocketknife.

Judy marched up to the table. She set down another mug of cocoa and two giant cinnamon buns, winked at Charlie, and marched off again.

"Thanks, Grandma!" Charlie called after her.

"How did the book get back to the library?" Fiona whispered, once Judy was out of earshot.

"Well, *I* didn't return it. My family didn't return it.

I knew that something strange was going on with that book, so I've been trying to keep track of it ever since."

"The same thing happened to me when *I* took the book home," Fiona breathed.

Charlie nodded, looking unsurprised.

Fiona wrapped one chilly hand around the cocoa mug. This boy had read the story. And, unlike Ms. Miranda, he seemed ready to believe that there *was* something hidden within it. Something he might help her find. "You said you know everything about this town."

Charlie nodded confidently. "I do."

"Then what really happened to Evelyn Chisholm?"

Charlie took a sip of cocoa. "That's the one thing I don't know."

Fiona lifted her own mug. Anybody who said there was only *one* thing he didn't know was almost definitely wrong.

"I know *basically* everything about this town," Charlie amended. "I know all the places and all the people. My family has been here forever. My grandpa and my great-grandpa were both named Charles Hobbes, and they both worked for the Chisholms. They've both passed on now. But my great-grandpa always said that Evelyn didn't die of an illness. He said something else happened, and the Chisholm family covered it up."

As hard as Fiona tried to focus on his words, the smell of cinnamon bun kept dragging her mind in another direction. "So . . . what happened?" she asked, through a giant mouthful.

"He wasn't sure." Charlie cut his own cinnamon bun into bite-sized pieces. "He just said she disappeared."

"Hey," said Fiona, swallowing so fast she nearly choked. "Do you think your great-grandpa wrote the book?"

"No." Charlie shook his head hard. "He grew up with the Chisholms. He was practically part of the family. He hated all the gossip about them. Plus, he wasn't really the book type." Charlie shrugged. "I'm the outlier in my family in that way."

Fiona took another huge bite. "Then who *did* write it?"

"Whoever did it was really angry at the Chisholms. Because that book is obviously cursed."

Fiona frowned. "Cursed?"

"Don't you know about curses?" Charlie gave her a look. "The book is cursed to remain at the library. It can't leave, not for long. Just like a ghost can't leave the place it haunts. And it doesn't even have an ending. It's *stuck*. Cursed."

Fiona gave Charlie a look of her own.

This boy was odder than she'd thought. He might even be a kook, which was what her mom and dad called people who believed in unscientific things. Still, it was nice to sit in a booth in a warm diner, drinking cocoa and trying to solve a puzzle with a . . . well, not a friend. But something not one hundred miles away.

"Ms. Miranda said those stories are just rumors," said Fiona at last. "She says Evelyn died of pneumonia or something, and people just spread gossip and conspiracy theories because that's what people in small towns do."

"Ms. Miranda isn't from here," said Charlie, as though this explained everything.

"Okay. Then . . ." Fiona took another gulp of cocoa, hoping not to sound like a kook herself. "Do you think the Searcher might be real?"

"Of course I do," said Charlie. "I'm *from* here."

"Plus there's the dog. The one that might be Pixie."

Charlie frowned. "Who else would it be?"

They were definitely in kook territory now. "You mean . . . you believe in ghosts?"

"Ghosts are just parts of the past that haven't stopped happening," said Charlie. "Things that are unfinished. Like if you disappeared, and no one ever found you."

No one ever found you. The words lingered like a scar in Fiona's mind.

What Charlie was saying made a strange kind of sense. Fiona believed in history, after all—in the traces that the past could leave behind. Traces like Evelyn Rose Chisholm.

"Ms. Miranda said the story wasn't true," said Fiona slowly. "But there's so much of it that *is* true. Margaret and Evelyn and your great-grandpa. Parson's Bridge. Evelyn's knife. Pixie."

"I know." Charlie nodded. "I think the whole story is true. I think the book is just waiting for someone to unlock the ending."

"But . . ." Fiona tapped her fork on her plate, thinking hard. "But Evelyn didn't disappear, like the book says. She died. There was a funeral. She has a gravestone in the cemetery."

Charlie nodded. "I know. I've seen it. It doesn't mean she's actually buried there."

"No," said Fiona, craning forward. "I just remembered. There's something weird about the stone."

"I know," said Charlie again. "I've *seen* it."

"You say that a lot," Fiona exploded.

"Say what?"

"'I know'!"

"I know." Charlie cracked a smile—the first one she had seen him wear. "I'm an obnoxious know-it-all. Everybody says so."

"Oh." Fiona gave him a smaller smile back. "Well. At least you know."

They both sipped their cocoa.

"What were you saying?" Charlie asked. "About the gravestone?"

"All the other Chisholm stones have dates, but there are no dates on Evelyn's. What if that's because they lied about her death? About when and how it happened?"

"That's a good theory. Or maybe there's no date because she was never buried at all."

Fiona tipped her head to the side. "You've thought about this already, haven't you?"

"A little." The expression on Charlie's face was less confident now. It was almost shy. "But it's nice to have someone to talk to about it. Finally."

Fiona scraped up a streak of icing with her fork. "Okay. Assuming *The Lost One* is true, how do we find the ending?"

"I know," said Charlie eagerly. "Well—I *might* know. We should search Evelyn's bedroom."

"You know about Evelyn's bedroom?"

"Of course I know about Evelyn's bedroom."

"Because you're *from here*?"

"No. Because I'm a know-it-all." Charlie flashed her another smile. "Let's go."

"Just a second," Fiona murmured as she and Charlie Hobbes stepped through the library's double doors.

"When I went up to Evelyn's room before, I got kicked out by one of the librarians who works up there. We should find out if she's up there right now."

Charlie nodded. "You should tell Ms. Miranda that you have a question for that other librarian. If she's here, they'll call her down, and if she isn't, we can sneak up right now."

"Yes," said Fiona. "Exactly." It was a little irritating, working with someone who knew everything already, but it did save a lot of explaining time.

They hurried toward the circulation desk.

Ms. Miranda looked up at them. Her dark hair was swept into an extra-elaborate heap this morning, with two tiny paper airplanes landing in its whorls. She gave a widening smile.

"Good morning, Fiona. And how's it going, Charlie? You two have met?"

"Good morning," Fiona answered. "We were just wondering . . . you know that librarian who works on the third floor?"

Ms. Miranda's eyebrows quirked. "On the third floor?"

"Yes. I had a question for her. About something we talked about the other day," Fiona improvised, hoping her voice sounded steadier on the outside than it did from within.

Ms. Miranda's eyebrows drew closer together.

"There's no one on the library staff who works on the third floor. It's just archives," she said. "What did she look like?"

"She was tall. Like . . . taller than you. She had curly gray hair. White skin. Big shoulders. She was wearing a long dress."

Charlie gave Fiona a poke in the back. Fiona ignored it, because Ms. Miranda and her eyebrows were still staring straight at her.

"I don't know who that would be." Ms. Miranda turned to Mr. Owens, who was sorting books at the other end of the desk. "Do you, James?"

"She definitely worked here," Fiona pushed on. "She knew all about the library. She told me what rooms I couldn't go in."

Charlie gave her another annoying poke. "I know who it was," he hissed into her ear. "It's all right," he added loudly, grabbing Fiona's arm. "We'll figure things out ourselves."

Before Fiona could argue, he steered her around the corner of the new arrivals shelf.

"I know who it was," Charlie whispered again, once they were hidden from view.

"So?" Fiona whispered back. "Just *knowing* who—"

"Really tall," Charlie interrupted. "Big shoulders. *Long dress.*"

"Long dress," Fiona repeated. *"What?"*

Charlie stared at her. "Mrs. Rawlins."

Fiona let out a breath through her nose. "Mrs. Rawlins must have died a long time ago."

"Exactly."

"This woman wasn't a ghost. She wasn't even *like* a ghost. She was solid. She talked to me. She was a *real person.*"

"She *was* a real person." Charlie's eyes glowed like stained glass lamps. "She's part of a story without an ending. So she's stuck here too."

Fiona took another exasperated nose-breath. "Let's just sneak up to the third floor," she whispered. "If she stops us, you'll see that she's real, and if she doesn't, we can visit Evelyn's room. Come on."

The third-floor hallway was even more hushed and dim than on Fiona's first visit. The rainy day outside the windows sent only a faint gray haze through the windows, and the dampness in the air seemed to muffle every sound.

They stopped before the last door in the hallway. Gently Fiona turned the knob.

At first glance, Evelyn's bedroom looked just as it had before. Fiona and Charlie stood on the threshold, gazing around at the lace curtains, the cluttered vanity, the books and treasures still waiting for an owner who had never come back.

Fiona's eyes drifted across the empty bed.

"Charlie," she breathed. *"Look."*

Lying on the silk covers, its cover tinted a deeper shade of green by the dimness, was a book.

The Lost One.

Chapter Nineteen

Fiona and Charlie raced to the bed.

Fiona snatched up the book, gripping it tight. "But—I left this on my bed just a couple of hours ago."

"Like I said, it's cursed," said Charlie. "It can't leave this place for long. But it *wants* someone to find it."

Fiona dragged her eyes away from the book long enough to stare back at him. "You really believe that?"

"The book chose us," said Charlie, as confidently as if he was giving an answer in math class. "We both keep finding it, or it keeps finding us. We've both seen Pixie. We found the knife. Why *wouldn't* I believe it?"

Fiona flipped through the book's familiar pages, trying to think of a logical reply. Halfway through, she stopped, her breath catching.

"Charlie." She held up the open book. *"There are new pages."*

It was impossible. Books didn't just write themselves. Of course, they didn't usually move themselves from room to room in rambling old libraries or around whispery old towns, either.

"Let's read it," said Charlie logically.

They leaned over the open book.

Afterward, no matter who asked, Pearl was never able to answer questions about what she had been doing in the water at night.

As the days passed, the grand brick house grew quieter and quieter. Where once lively music had poured from a gramophone and songs had chimed from a grand piano, there were now closed lids and locked doors. Where staff had bustled upstairs and down, chatting in the kitchen, whistling in the yard, there were bowed heads and whispers and worried looks.

And where there had been the noise of two girls running, laughing, followed by a barking dog, there was nothing at all.

Meanwhile, outside the grand brick house, the search went on. The sheriff and deputies and an army of hired help combed the town. They knocked at farmhouse doors, examined tumbledown barns and rocky caves, tromped the far reaches of the woods behind a pack of leashed bloodhounds. But there was no trace of Hazel.

Until, at last, there was.

Fiona reached the bottom of the page. She could read faster than almost everyone she knew, and she was used to having to stop and wait for school partners to catch up. But when she glanced over at Charlie, she found him already looking back at her.

"You're done?" she asked.

"I finished a few seconds ago," said Charlie. "You can turn the page."

Fiona did. She read even faster now, wanting to know what happened next, and wanting to know it just before Charlie.

Though quiet had filled all the chambers of the grand brick house, nowhere was that quiet so complete as at the end of the third floor.

Hazel's bedroom was empty, of course. Pearl remained shut in the room next door, emerging more and more rarely. Mrs. Rawlins and Mrs. Fisher checked on her nearly every hour, bringing trays and tea, freshening bedding, and changing clothes.

For days, this routine persisted, until its abnormality had almost become normality. And then, one sunless afternoon, Mrs. Rawlins withdrew from the third-floor bedroom with an untouched tea tray in her arms and a haunted expression on her broad face. She hurried down the corridor so fast that Pixie, who had been sprawled listlessly on the floor outside Hazel's room, raised his head with a curious woof.

Mrs. Rawlins tapped at the door of the study, where the man and lady of the house were closed up together, writing a plea for information that would appear in newspapers all across New England.

"Ma'am?" Mrs. Rawlins called softly. "May I have a word?"

Minutes later, the girls' mother and the housekeeper climbed the stairs together, with tight lips and anxious eyes.

Mrs. Rawlins stood guard outside the bedroom door. Pixie lay at her feet.

When Pearl's mother emerged, her face was so bloodless it might have been sculpted of snow.

"Please call Father Carson," she told Mrs. Rawlins. "I must speak to my husband."

That evening, a long, murmured conversation tinged the silence of the house. Father Carson, Dr. O'Malley, and Mr. Bronty, the family's longtime attorney, remained locked in the study with the girls' parents until nearly midnight.

The door opened at last, sending the doctor and the attorney hurrying out of the house. Father Carson lingered, paying a brief visit to the quiet bedroom at the end of the third-floor hall. Then he too rushed out into the dark.

"Thank you, Mrs. Rawlins," said the man of the house, stepping out of the study to meet her in the great room. "You should retire for the night."

"Are you sure, sir?" Mrs. Rawlins asked. "I'm glad to wait up. I could bring a fresh pot of coffee or tea. . . ."

"No. Thank you." He clasped her on the shoulder. "We'll never be able to thank you for your kindness. And your loyalty."

Mrs. Rawlins still didn't depart. "Pearl. The poor child. Will she be all right?"

"It's the grief and shock of it all." Her employer shook his head. "She hardly knows what she's saying. After some more rest, we shall see. Now, Mrs. Rawlins." He managed the semblance of a smile. "Off to bed with you. I insist."

Mrs. Rawlins nodded.

There came the snap of a turning bolt as her employer withdrew into the study once more. Mrs. Rawlins turned toward the back staircase. But before departing, she caught the click of a lifting earpiece, and a low voice speaking into the telephone.

By morning, the joyful news had spread through half the town.

Hazel had come home.

"What?" Fiona whispered to herself, just a second before Charlie muttered, *"What?"*

They glanced at each other and whipped to the next page.

Of course the poor girl was exhausted.

She had been out in the elements for days, scrounging for food, sleeping in the cold and damp. It was no wonder she had a fever, or that she looked so thin and worn. For the time being, she would be shut in her room, tucked into bed, fed by Mrs. Fisher's broths and visited frequently by Dr. O'Malley.

All of this news the family put out themselves.

The other statements that spread through the town—that Hazel had run away from home just to give her parents an awful fright, that she was a reckless and spoiled girl who had wasted everybody's time, and that she was lucky the Searcher hadn't taken her after all—spread on their own, like seeds from a weed, growing faster and stronger than the tended plants around them.

Several days passed. The hush that filled the grand brick house changed only slightly, from one of shock to one of illness and worry.

A new rumor began to travel the town: Hazel's fever, contracted during those long days and nights of exposure, had worsened. The doctor's car was seen in the drive of the quiet brick house at least once each day. To prevent contagion and too much excitement, only he, the girl's parents, and Mrs. Rawlins were allowed into Hazel's room.

Charlie Hobbes tried to visit her once, creeping up the stairs with an eagle feather and a bright-winged moth in a jar, but he was caught and turned away by the stalwart Mrs. Rawlins.

"Can you at least give these to Hazel?" he asked, passing over the gifts.

Mrs. Rawlins sighed and held out her hands. She gave Charlie a look that was softer than usual. "I will," she promised. "You go on now."

Charlie hurried back down the stairs. The gift he would have most liked to bring to Hazel was her own pocketknife, still hidden in the soil beneath the oak tree. But it was Pearl who had hidden it, and he knew better than to get himself into the middle of a battle between the sisters. Besides, Pearl would surely return it eventually.

This is what Charlie told himself as he stepped out of the house onto the back lawn. He was only a moment too late to see Mrs. Rawlins opening a third-floor window and releasing a moth into the June air.

Another day ticked by.

The house, impossibly, grew quieter still, as though every door and wall and window was holding its breath. One more bit of news slipped across its threshold.

Hazel had succumbed to the fever, and died.

And died. And died. And died.

The words repeated again and again, to the bottom of the page.

Fiona flipped forward, not even checking to see if Charlie had kept up this time. The rest of the pages were still blank.

"So . . . it was a lie, right?" Fiona whispered to Charlie, her throat tight. "Hazel didn't really come home at all."

Charlie shook his head, still staring down at the pages. "The family just *pretended* she did."

"And they got everybody else to pretend, too. But *why*?"

Charlie didn't answer. Which meant he didn't know.

Fiona brushed her fingers over the dusty bed. The bed where Evelyn Chisholm hadn't died after all.

"Hey," she said, barely able to believe the unscientific things heading out of her own mouth. "What if the book only tells the whole story if it trusts the person reading it? What if that's why we found it in the first place, and that's why it's showing us more of the story now? Because it thinks we'll understand?"

Charlie looked thoughtful. "That's an interesting theory," he said. "And if someone, or something, can move the book, it makes sense that it could alter the book too."

They stood side by side in the hush for a moment.

"What do we do now?" Fiona asked, thinking aloud. "Do we take the book with us, or—"

"I think we should leave it right here," said Charlie. "This is where it came on its own. This is where new pages appeared."

Fiona nodded. "Maybe if we leave it here, it will happen again." She closed the book, letting her fingers slide across the soft leather cover. She thought of the archeologists who discovered sacred things, like graves and temples and relics, and who decided to leave them where they'd been placed. Because the past deserved respect.

She reached into her pocket.

"This belongs here too." She set the knife on the closed book.

Charlie nodded. "I'm sure Evelyn . . ."

But he didn't finish. Because the pocketknife had begun to move.

It wobbled on its rounded handle like an egg set on a countertop. As Fiona and Charlie stared, it spun faster and faster, making several full circles before coming back to a halt.

"The—the floor must be uneven," said Fiona shakily, grasping for explanations. "Or there's a draft or something."

"Do you hear that?" Charlie whispered.

His eyes went from the knife to the far side of the room—to the spot where the knife's handle was pointing.

The spot where a peephole was drilled through the wall.

They both dashed toward it.

Charlie got there first. "Look," he breathed, leaning to the side.

Fiona squinted through the tiny opening.

On the other side was a room that looked very much like the one where they stood now, with gilt-framed pictures, a carved wooden vanity and dresser, and a silk-blanketed bed.

But someone was lying in that bed.

As Fiona stared, holding her breath, she saw the silky blankets stir, and heard the sound of a girl's voice, quietly, brokenly, sobbing.

Fiona and Charlie raced out of Evelyn's bedroom. They skidded toward the next door in the hall. Fiona yanked it open.

The room beyond was empty.

Chapter Twenty

Fiona and Charlie stared into the dimness.

The glow of light was gone. The furniture and pictures and silk bedding were gone. And the figure in the bed was gone as completely as if it had never been there.

"But I *saw* her," said Fiona, half to herself. "I *heard* her."

She rushed back into Evelyn's room and pressed her face to the peephole, Charlie right behind. The room beyond remained dark and empty.

"This doesn't make sense," Fiona muttered.

"Yes, it does," Charlie answered, in his most know-it-all way.

Fiona spun toward him. *"How?"*

"Like you said yourself, the book chose us. It must be trying to tell us something else."

"Like what?"

"I don't know," said Charlie, after a begrudging pause. But then he added, "*Yet*. We just need time to figure it out."

"Well, we don't have extra time right now." Fiona took a step backward. "I have to get home before my family does. And we have to get out of here before any librarians find us."

"I know what we should do," said Charlie as they crept back along the hall. "We should come back here tonight. After the library is closed."

"After it's closed?" Fiona glanced at him.

Charlie's eyes had started to glow again. "So we can check the book and see if there's more to the story. And we can explore the whole building with nobody stopping us. Plus, apparitions are more likely to appear after dark. I've read half of the paranormal section in this place. I *know*."

"How are we going to get inside? Do you have a key?"

"We don't need one. We'll both go home and act like everything is normal. Then I'll sneak back here right before closing, during the dinner rush at the diner, and hide inside when the librarians leave."

Fiona paused at the top of the third-floor staircase. "You think that will work?"

"If I'm careful. I'll open the door for you, and we'll have the whole night to look around."

Fiona folded her arms, considering. "I won't be able to sneak out until my family is asleep. They all go to bed pretty early, though."

"Can you meet me here at ten?"

"Ten," Fiona repeated slowly. "Ten should work."

She and Charlie nodded to each other. Then, as quietly as they could, they crept back down the STAFF ONLY stairs.

That night, after the sky had turned from deep blue to black, Fiona inched through her bedroom door.

It had been an ordinary evening at home. The Crane family had eaten dinner together before scattering in separate directions. If anybody had noticed that Fiona was more distracted and jumpy than usual, they didn't say so. And no one, Fiona included, noticed that Arden was quieter than usual too.

By nine thirty, they had all been closed in their bedrooms, leaving the old colonial house dim and quiet. Now the squeak of the stairs under Fiona's feet was the only sound.

She stopped in the hallway to adjust her backpack. The flashlight and spare batteries inside clicked softly. Swinging it back over her shoulder, she padded past the kitchen, past the living-room doors and—

Someone was in the living room.

Fiona froze in the doorway.

The figure was sitting on the couch, still and silent. No lights were on, and the moonlight that pushed its way through the wobbly glassed windows wasn't strong enough for her to see it clearly. But it had a human shape, with thin arms and hunched shoulders and a head that swiveled to face her. Something glowed faintly in its hand.

The screen of a smartphone.

"Arden?" Fiona squeaked.

"Oh my gosh. You scared me." Arden gasped back. "Why are you creeping around down here in the dark?"

"Why are *you*?" Fiona countered.

Arden dropped the phone to her lap, its glow lighting the edges of her face. "I couldn't sleep. I wanted to watch a few videos and work on things without waking Mom and Dad."

Fiona craned toward the phone. On its screen, a miniature Arden whirled silently around an ice rink. Arden tapped a button, and the video disappeared.

Thicker darkness filled the room.

The darkness came too late, though. Arden could have already noticed the backpack over Fiona's shoulder, and the sweatshirt and shoes she was wearing.

There was no point in Fiona saying she had just come downstairs for a glass of water.

But before she could settle on an excuse, Arden sniffled. She brushed her cheek with a shirt cuff, turning her face away.

"Were you crying?" Fiona asked.

"No," said Arden, in a congested voice.

"Yes, you were. You still sound all sniffly."

"Being at the rink all day makes my nose run. You know that."

"Does it make your eyes water too?"

Arden threw herself back against the couch cushions. "I'm *fine*, Fiona. Go back to bed."

"You're not fine." Fiona slipped the backpack strap from her shoulder and lowered it to the floor beside the couch, hoping her sister hadn't seen it after all. If she could just get Arden to go upstairs, she should still be able to slip out. "If you were fine, you'd be asleep right now. Aren't you supposed to get nine hours of sleep a night when you're training? That's what Mom always says."

"Yes, I'm *supposed* to," said Arden. "There are lots of things I'm *supposed* to be doing right now."

"So maybe you should at least try to rest. Not just sit there watching videos of yourself."

Arden made a sound that was a mixture of a snort

and a mean laugh. But then she sniffed again. Fiona saw her swipe a hand over her eyes, quickly, like she was hoping Fiona wouldn't catch it.

"What's wrong?" Fiona asked, growing impatient. "Did you only get second place at that last competition or something?"

Arden gave another snort. "The Longfellow Open? I didn't even place."

"You didn't?" Fiona absorbed most things about Arden's life just by being present, smacked by the constant waves of figure-skating talk like an anemone in a tide pool. She must not have been listening when her family discussed this competition. Or maybe Arden hadn't wanted to talk about this one. "What happened?"

"I just didn't skate well, okay? The judges didn't like my new program. It wasn't smooth enough or heartfelt enough or whatever, and I had to skate right after the girl who ended up taking first in the whole thing, and Mom wasn't even there, and I'd just had that stupid fight with you, and I missed *two* jumps, and I've been doing horribly at everything ever since we moved here. That's what happened."

Fiona thought of the untied knot in the skate lace. The medal hidden under Arden's bed. The tiny things she'd done to counter the big thing Arden had done.

"What do you mean, since we moved here? I thought you *wanted* to move here."

"Mom and Dad wanted to move," said Arden. "And yeah, it's nice to be closer to the rink. But . . . I don't know."

"What?" Fiona pushed.

"I don't want to talk about this, okay?" Arden sagged forward on the couch, and a faint beam of moonlight through the latticed windows brushed her face. Her cheeks were wet. Her hair was mussed. "Just leave me alone, Fiona."

"But . . . you're sad," said Fiona.

And she had *wanted* Arden to be sad. She'd wanted Arden to feel a tiny bit of what she felt herself. So why was there a cold, tugging sensation, like a needle with a long steel thread, twisting through her heart right now?

"But I *shouldn't* be sad," said Arden. "Because it's my fault. We moved here because of me. To this weird old house in this creepy little town, with some *Searcher* maybe wandering through the woods, and now everything's going wrong, but I shouldn't say anything about it, especially not to you, because it's my own fault."

At least Arden was blaming the right person, Fiona thought. She glanced at the window, wondering what time it was by now. She couldn't be so late that Charlie gave up on her and scrapped their whole plan. But she couldn't bolt out the door right in front of her sister, either.

Her *crying* sister.

"Well, it's like Dad says," Fiona told Arden. "New things just take some getting used to. I'm sure you'll feel back to normal soon."

"By then it will be too late." Arden wiped her nose on her sleeve.

Fiona couldn't believe that perfect Arden was wiping nose drips on her own clothes. "Too late for what?"

"Everything." Arden flung out her hands. "For my whole career."

"You're thirteen," said Fiona.

"I *know!*" Arden burst out. "For a skater, that's not young. Skaters have a certain number of years. *Competitive* years. I messed up the Longfellow Open. I'm still not nailing my new program. Even my practice sessions are sloppy. Carolyn thinks—" She stopped, her voice catching. "Carolyn thinks I might not be ready for my next test. But I need to pass that test to move up to junior level, so I can get to *senior* level, or I'm never going to make it *at all*."

"Make it to what?"

"To Nationals. To the Olympics. To a career." Arden swiped the tears from her eyes. "It will all just fall apart."

Fiona had seen Arden's meltdowns many times. She'd seen her scream over ill-fitting skate boots, costumes the wrong color, mean whispers from other skaters. But she'd never seen her sister look so . . . what was it? *Defeated.* That's how she looked now.

Arden, who won everything.

The tugging in Fiona's heart pulled harder.

"Arden, you don't *have* to make it to the Olympics."

"If I don't, then what was all of this for? All the years of practicing. All the money Mom and Dad spent. Making everybody move here. Making you hate me."

"I don't hate you," Fiona murmured.

Maybe she said it too softly. Because Arden's face crumpled.

"I just feel like—" she began. "I feel like everything is piled up on top of me. And I'm dropping it. I'm failing." Arden buried her wet face in her hands.

Fiona watched her sister for a moment. Then she stepped forward, placing one hand awkwardly on Arden's shoulder.

Arden stiffened. Fiona's hand fell away.

"Forget I said anything," said Arden. "I'm fine. I'm fine." She sniffled once more, brushing the hair back from her face. She whipped toward Fiona. "You never said what *you* were doing down here."

Fiona stepped backward. "I couldn't sleep either."

"But you had your backpack." Arden's eyes narrowed. "Were you going to sneak out again? *At night?*"

"No," said Fiona, futilely.

"There's something weird going on with you," said Arden, holding Fiona with the spear points of her eyes. "Ever since we moved here, you've been all secretive and obsessive. Even more than usual, I mean. It has to do with that library, doesn't it? Tell me the truth, or I'll tell Mom and Dad about you sneaking out the other day."

Fiona rocked on her feet, wishing she could think of any other way out. "If I tell you, you can't tell them about tonight, either."

"I'm not promising. Not until I know what you're doing." Arden leaned forward on the cushions. "So tell, or I'm going up to wake Mom and Dad right now."

"Okay. *Okay.*" Fiona swallowed, trying to sort her thoughts into two shareable and secret piles. "I found this book. . . ."

She gave Arden the short and simple version; the one where Fiona read *The Lost One*, figured out that it was set in Lost Lake, and began to uncover its missing ending with the help of a new friend. She left out the book's strange movements, and the pocketknife, and the fact that she and Charlie were hoping more of its pages would inexplicably appear. The less Arden knew, the less she could tell.

"So," said Arden, when she'd finished, "you're going to sneak out of the house after dark, when you're already in trouble, to break into a closed library?" She stared at Fiona. "That is the *worst* idea."

"We're not breaking in," said Fiona.

"Seriously?" Arden gestured at the darkness outside the windows. "It's not even *safe*, with the Searcher, or who knows what, waiting out there in this weird place."

"The Searcher isn't real," said Fiona, before she could rethink the words.

Arden blinked. "You said it was."

"No, I didn't. I just said other people said it was," Fiona answered impatiently. "I was just trying to scare you."

Arden frowned. "Why?"

"Because! Because you made us move here. Because I wanted you to think that maybe there was something wrong with this place. Then you'd at least feel bad for dragging everybody else here along with you."

"You think I don't already feel bad?" Arden stood up. She gazed down at Fiona for a moment. "You've been messing up my room, haven't you?" she asked softly. "So I'd be scared. So I'd think there was something wrong. Did you untie the knot in my lace too?"

Even in the dimness, Fiona couldn't meet her sister's eyes. She looked at the scarred hardwood floor, gray-blue as ice in the moonlight. The two of them might as well have been standing on a frozen lake.

"You just had to tie it again," said Fiona, very quietly.

"I can't believe . . ." Arden's voice was quiet too. "Never mind," she said, more clearly. "It doesn't even matter. Just leave. Go out in the dark all by yourself. I'm not going to tell." She stepped past Fiona, into the hallway.

"Arden." Fiona still couldn't meet her sister's eyes. "I'm sorry."

"It doesn't matter," said Arden again. "You know what? I hope the Searcher finds you."

She turned and padded away, her footsteps nearly silent on the ancient wooden floor.

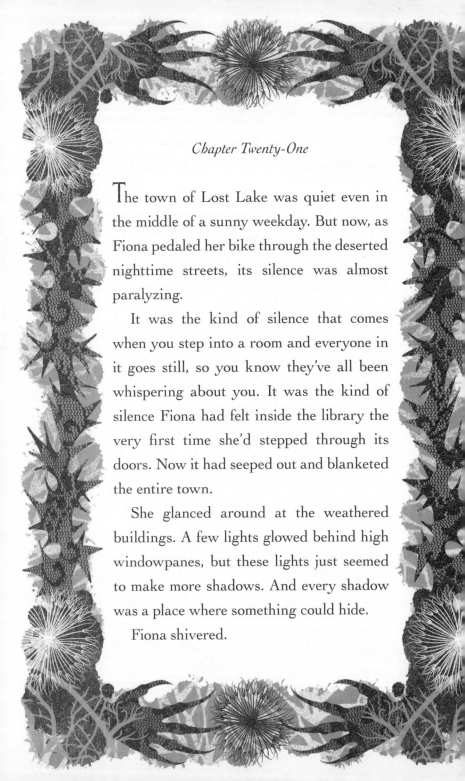

Chapter Twenty-One

The town of Lost Lake was quiet even in the middle of a sunny weekday. But now, as Fiona pedaled her bike through the deserted nighttime streets, its silence was almost paralyzing.

It was the kind of silence that comes when you step into a room and everyone in it goes still, so you know they've all been whispering about you. It was the kind of silence Fiona had felt inside the library the very first time she'd stepped through its doors. Now it had seeped out and blanketed the entire town.

She glanced around at the weathered buildings. A few lights glowed behind high windowpanes, but these lights just seemed to make more shadows. And every shadow was a place where something could hide.

Fiona shivered.

They were just shadows, she told herself. There was no Searcher. Even though her sister had wished for the Searcher to find her. Even though something had followed Margaret Chisholm through the narrow old streets of this town a hundred years ago. Even though something dark and tall and quiet had just billowed across the edge of her vision—

Fiona whipped around, nearly toppling her bike.

A flag hanging from a nearby porch furled and unfurled in the breeze.

Fiona swallowed.

She wouldn't let Arden scare her.

Even though she had tried to scare Arden first.

Fiona pushed this thought aside, straightened her bike, and flew onward, toward the library.

"I thought you weren't going to come," Charlie whispered, opening the front doors wide enough for Fiona to slip inside.

"My sister almost stopped me," Fiona whispered back. "Sorry I'm late."

Charlie closed the library doors behind her.

The darkness of the night outside was nothing compared to the moonless black inside the old house. It made every sound seem louder, sharper, the way a black stage curtain sets off a spotlight.

"Where are the light switches?" Fiona asked, groping for the wall.

"We can't turn the lights on," Charlie answered. "Someone outside could see. But I brought this."

There was a click. Something purplish and about the size of a cauliflower flared to life in Charlie's hands.

Fiona blinked into the cloud of light. "What is that?"

"A night-light." Charlie held up a purple plastic octopus with eight glowing arms and a smiling head. "It lights a wider area than a flashlight does. I don't use it anymore," he added, a bit defensively. "And if you just click the button once, it doesn't play any music."

Fiona felt herself start to smile. "I wonder if anybody ever snuck into a library to solve a mystery with a glowing octopus before."

The purplish light revealed Charlie smiling back. "I think the odds are low."

Fiona looked around the huge central chamber. Armchairs and deserted desks formed shadowy hulks. Doorways to other, even darker, rooms gaped like open mouths. The size of this place, and of the task ahead of them, tumbled down on her all at once. "Ready?" she asked, in a voice that was far more fragile than she wanted it to be.

Charlie nodded. "Ready."

They scurried up the central staircase. As they

passed, the night-light's glow struck the portrait of grown-up Margaret Chisholm. Her painted eyes glittered at them before fading back into the darkness.

Evelyn's room was just as they had left it: hushed and eerie, waiting for someone who had never returned. *The Lost One* and the pocketknife still lay on the bed.

Fiona dove for the book. "Charlie," she breathed, opening it. "There's more of the story."

"I knew it." Charlie set the octopus on the bedside table. "It *wants* to tell us the truth."

"Maybe," Fiona whispered back, barely able to push the word past her thudding heartbeat.

They bent over the open book.

After a small funeral attended by only the immediate family and Mrs. Rawlins, and after a similarly swift and private interment in the family's cemetery plot, the grand brick house entered a period of mourning.

One it never left.

The house stood quietly amid its towering trees as summer's flowers withered, as oak leaves browned and fell, as frost whitened the surrounding ground. Quiet weeks turned to quiet months, and finally to quiet years.

The man and woman of the house, always fond of travel, spent increasing spans of time away. Eventually they went abroad by ocean liner, taking so many trunks and cases that it was clear they might never return at all.

The neighbors tutted with sympathy. Naturally the place bore too many painful reminders. And if Pearl had been less delicate, her parents would surely have taken her along.

But they did not.

Pearl remained at home, under the care of Mrs. Rawlins. With Mr. Hobbes and Charlie to maintain the place, and Mrs. Rawlins and Mrs. Fisher to run it, the house managed to keep a faint air of its former elegance, or at least of respectability. And yet only a glance at its curtained windows, its empty lawns, and its dozens of unused, unlit rooms told passersby a fragment of the story concealed inside.

As for Pearl, she grew up.

She did it alone but for the paid help that had always surrounded her. She became a young woman, and then a woman who was no longer called young. She left the house less and less, and fewer and fewer guests stepped through its doors.

Her parents passed away while still abroad and were brought home to rest in the family plot, next to Hazel's stone. Mr. Hobbes passed on, and Mrs. Fisher, and finally Mrs. Rawlins too, until there was no one left who remembered what Pearl had whispered to Mrs. Rawlins after Hazel's disappearance.

Mrs. Rawlins certainly never forgot it; not for as long as she lived. She never forgot Pearl's pale face and wide, haunted eyes, or the broken sound of her voice as she whispered, "Mrs. Rawlins . . . the Searcher was a lie. *I* killed her."

I killed her. I killed her. I killed her.

The awful words echoed down the remainder of the page.

The next page—one of a very small number now—stayed blank.

Fiona and Charlie sat still.

The ancient mattress sagged beneath them, pressing their shoulders together. Fiona wasn't sure if the shaking she felt came from Charlie or from her.

Fiona clasped her fingers tight together. *No.* She wouldn't believe it. It couldn't really be Margaret's fault. Evelyn was the one who had started it all. Evelyn was to blame.

"What do you think it means?" she whispered, glancing at Charlie. "What do you think really happened?"

Charlie nodded at the pocketknife lying on the bedspread. "Maybe that's why she buried the knife."

Fiona stiffened. No. *No.* Margaret couldn't have done *that*.

"What about the Searcher?" she asked instead. "She

219

didn't say it wasn't real. She said the Searcher was a lie. What do you think she meant?"

Charlie didn't answer. Which meant he didn't know.

"We must still be missing something," Fiona whispered.

Charlie nodded. "Plus, there are still blank pages. This isn't the end."

"So . . . whoever is telling the story . . ." Fiona suppressed a small shiver. "How do we get them to finish it?"

Again, Charlie didn't answer.

"Hey, Charlie?" Fiona asked, after a moment. "Why are we whispering?"

"Because this is a library," he whispered back.

"But there's nobody else here."

Charlie paused for a second before answering, still in a whisper, "We both know that can't be true."

They were quiet for another heartbeat.

And then, from somewhere far below, there came the thud of a closing door.

Chapter Twenty-Two

Fiona and Charlie darted to the bedroom doorway.

The third-floor hallway remained deserted and dark. But from a distance there came another sound, like heavy footsteps stalking across a floor.

Side by side, Charlie gripping the night-light, they padded along the corridor to the stairs.

They had just reached the second-floor walkway when the lights of the central chamber flashed on. Fiona reeled back into the staircase alcove, half blinded. Charlie nearly lost his grip on the night-light.

"Charlie?" shouted a voice. "Charlie!"

"Uh-oh," Charlie breathed, a look of defeat washing over his face. *"Grandma."*

"Charlie Hobbes!" the voice blared.

"You're sure he's here?" asked another familiar voice.

Fiona and Charlie crept toward the banister. Below them, in the central chamber, stood Judy Hobbes and Ms. Miranda.

Fiona's heart cannonballed into her stomach.

"Oh, I'm sure." Judy stalked across the room toward the grand staircase. *"CHARLIE!"*

Charlie whirled toward Fiona. "You should stay here," he whispered. "Don't waste our chance."

"What if Ms. Miranda guesses I'm here anyway?" Fiona whispered back.

"Charlie?" Judy's heavy steps creaked up the stairs. "If you can hear me, you had better answer!"

Charlie shoved the night-light into Fiona's hands. "Up here, Grandma!" he shouted back. Before Fiona could argue, he took off toward the staircase.

Fiona clicked off the light.

"Charlie Hobbes." Judy stopped on the third step, her fists on her hips. "Do you know how many rules you're breaking?"

"Yes, I know." Charlie climbed very slowly down the steps.

"What were you thinking, breaking into the library after hours?"

"I didn't break in," said Charlie. "I just *stayed* in."

Judy huffed like a hot teakettle. "Well, why did you *stay* in?"

Fiona glanced from Judy to Ms. Miranda. The librarian's sharp brown eyes were fixed on Charlie too.

Charlie reached the foot of the steps before answering. "I've been rereading *From the Mixed-Up Files of Mrs. Basil E. Frankweiler*, where the main characters hide out in the Metropolitan Museum of Art. I wanted to try something like that myself."

"No you don't, Charlie," said Ms. Miranda, with a dry smile. "You don't get to blame a book for this." Her eyes moved past Charlie, up the stairs, along the walkway.

Fiona huddled lower.

"Oh, I'm not blaming the book," said Charlie. "I'm just saying that sometimes it feels like a book is speaking right to you. Remember what you said during the summer reading program last year? That there's a right book for every reader, and a right reader for every book?"

Ms. Miranda looked at Charlie, her eyes sharp and bright as a spotlight. "I remember," she said slowly.

"How did you know where I was, Grandma?" Charlie asked, turning back toward Judy.

"Oh, you're not hard to find. When school's out, if you're not at home or at the diner, you're *here*." His grandma wrapped a forceful arm around Charlie's shoulders. "Now apologize to Ms. Miranda, or you'll be spending *all* of your time helping out at the Perch."

"I'm sorry, Ms. Miranda," said Charlie. "I'd understand why you might have to ban me from the library. Although I hope you won't."

"Well," said Ms. Miranda, with a very small smile. "Since it was a one-time thing, and since you did it on your own . . . I think we can move on. Just this once."

"Lucky for you." Judy steered Charlie toward the doors. "Home. Now."

From behind them, Ms. Miranda aimed one more look at the second-floor walkway.

Fiona froze against the banister, not breathing, not even blinking. For a sliver of a second, she could have sworn that Ms. Miranda's eyes landed on her.

But the librarian turned away. There was the click of a switch as the lights went out, plunging the library back into darkness. The double doors thumped shut.

Fiona was alone.

She leaned hard against the banister, her panting breaths filling the dark. It was all right, she told herself. Darkness couldn't hurt you. Being alone couldn't hurt you either.

She forced herself to count to twenty. When she was sure it was safe, she switched Charlie's night-light back on.

The octopus glowed cheerily.

Inside its cloud of light, Fiona wobbled to her feet. Charlie was right. She shouldn't waste this chance. After tonight, she might be grounded forever and never get another one. Besides, archeologists didn't let darkness and strange sounds scare them away. They climbed into tombs, through underground tunnels, down ancient stone stairways.

She could do this. She *had* to do it. Charlie was relying on her. Maybe Margaret was too.

She could do it by herself.

Clutching the glowing octopus, Fiona rushed up the stairs and down the hall to Evelyn's bedroom. One glance through the door told her two things.

Both *The Lost One* and the pocketknife were gone.

And she definitely wasn't alone in this house.

Chapter Twenty-Three

Fiona wavered on the threshold, gripping the glowing octopus with both hands.

She scanned the floor, just in case the missing things had simultaneously fallen from their places.

They hadn't.

Someone had taken them.

She and Charlie had left this room just minutes ago. No one had passed them on the third-floor staircase. Which meant whoever it was had to be nearby.

And now whoever it was had a knife.

All rational thoughts flew out of Fiona's brain like a flock of birds in front of an incoming airplane.

She barreled back down the hallway, half expecting something—a ghost, a knife-wielding stranger, a hunched black-cloaked terror—to lunge at her through the surrounding doors.

She thundered down the creaky stairs. It didn't matter if she kept quiet anymore. Whoever was here already knew about her too.

She skidded onto the second-floor walkway. Moonlight through the tall, narrow windows brightened the air, glazing the central room with foggy gray. She was almost to the main staircase. She was almost on her way out.

Fiona wheeled onto the staircase landing.

But someone was already there.

A girl.

A girl with long brown hair, a pleated ivory dress, and a green leather-bound book in her hands. A girl who was staring at the portrait of Margaret Chisholm. Next to her, its body quivering with excitement, sat a curly brown dog.

Fiona stopped so abruptly that she almost fell on her face. She threw out a hand, catching herself on the banister and dropping the octopus night-light. There was a thunking crack as its light winked out.

The girl turned.

Fiona stared.

Long brown hair. Old-fashioned dress. A face as pale and misty as ice. Pixie sitting beside her.

It would have been easier if both sisters had been there, so she could compare them: taller, shorter, older, younger, the way people did with her and Arden. But the soft face and dreamy eyes made her sure—as sure as she could be about something so impossible—that she was looking at Margaret Chisholm.

"Hello," Fiona breathed.

The girl stared back at her with eyes that were gray and steady. "Hello." Her voice was like the creaks of the floor, or the soft rush of night wind against the walls.

Pixie glanced back and forth between the two of them, bristly nose twitching.

The girl turned back to the portrait. "This doesn't belong here. Who is this?"

"Th-that?" Fiona's voice stuck on the word. "That's Margaret Chisholm."

A strange expression crossed the girl's face. She stared at the portrait again, eyes wide, eyebrows drawn together.

"You're Margaret Chisholm too," Fiona whispered. "Aren't you?"

The girl's eyes flicked from the portrait back to Fiona. And Fiona saw something else in them now. Something anxious and hopeful and lonely. Something that was waiting to be recognized.

"My name is Fiona Crane." Fiona pushed on, as steadily as she could. "I—I've read that book. I know what happened."

The girl's face seemed to tighten. "You do?"

"Well . . . I don't know *everything*." Fiona inched forward, fighting the wobble in her knees. "I haven't read the ending yet. But I know you couldn't really have hurt your sister."

A new expression flickered over the girl's face. Wariness. Maybe even fear. She gripped the book, pulling back.

"You could tell me the truth right now," Fiona persisted. "You could tell me what *really* happened. That's why you and the book and Pixie and everything are stuck, isn't it? Because nobody knows the whole story. Except you."

The girl seemed to waver like the flame on a candle. "The book is . . . it was just for me. And for . . . for her." She clutched the book with shaking fingers. "I thought it might help. I thought if I turned it all into a story . . . it might be easier to believe."

"Wait. *You* wrote the book?" Fiona's thoughts tumbled and slid, rearranging themselves. "But that means it's *not* just a story. Because you know what really happened. At the end."

"But I couldn't . . . even on paper, I couldn't . . ." Margaret's voice thinned. "I erased that part," she whispered. "No one else was ever supposed to know."

"Until now." Fiona rushed to finish Margaret's

thought. "But you knew we'd understand. That's why you've been moving the book around, isn't it? So we would find it, and you could finally tell the right person the whole truth?" She held out one hand. "Can I read the rest now? Please, Margaret. I'm on your side. I swear."

But Margaret Chisholm stepped out of her reach again. "I never moved the book."

Fiona halted. "You didn't?"

Margaret shook her head. "That is—I only moved it *back*. I always brought it back here, back up to her room, where it belonged. Where it would be safe."

Fiona stared at the trembling girl. "Then . . . who . . ."

Pixie let out a howl.

The sound pierced the air, slicing through Fiona's words, ringing away through the empty rooms. Fiona's skin tightened with goosebumps.

Margaret spun away. She stared, petrified, down the staircase.

The library's double doors thumped open.

On the threshold, outlined by moonlight, loomed a black-cloaked figure.

A wave of horror crashed through Fiona's heart.

The Searcher stepped forward. Its cloak dragged along the parquet. Its hood was too deep to reveal any hint of a face inside—if there was a face at all—but

Fiona could sense something within that hood staring back at them both, holding them still with its invisible eyes.

No. *The Searcher is a lie.* Margaret had said so herself, in the book.

But when Fiona managed to turn her head just enough to catch the other girl with the corner of her eye, Margaret's expression was pure terror, her face as pale and stiff as stone.

The Searcher took another step. A rush of cold air swept up the staircase, carrying the smell of damp and mud and rot.

"But it's not real," Fiona choked out, not sure who she was speaking to. "It isn't real."

The Searcher came closer still. Slowly. Slowly, as though it wanted them to wait. It wanted their dread.

Pixie gave a strangled whimper.

The Searcher reached the base of the stairs.

It set its weight on the bottom step. Fiona couldn't glimpse a foot or a leg or anything human about it, but she thought she saw a small pool of dark water forming there, a puddle in place of a footprint. A glittering trail marked its path across the parquet.

The Searcher began to climb.

Margaret whipped toward Fiona. She thrust the book into Fiona's shaky hands.

"Run," she whispered, before turning and vanishing into the darkness.

For one fragment of a second, Fiona wavered in place, gripping the book. Then, without knowing where she was going or what she would do when she got there, Fiona whirled around in the opposite direction, and ran.

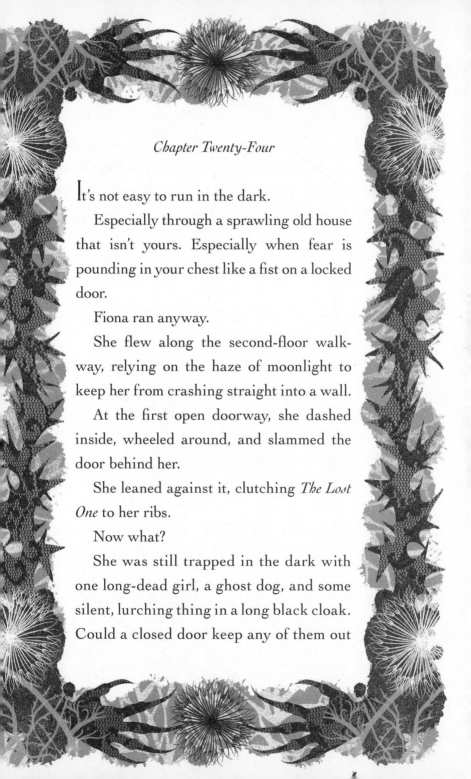

Chapter Twenty-Four

It's not easy to run in the dark.

Especially through a sprawling old house that isn't yours. Especially when fear is pounding in your chest like a fist on a locked door.

Fiona ran anyway.

She flew along the second-floor walkway, relying on the haze of moonlight to keep her from crashing straight into a wall.

At the first open doorway, she dashed inside, wheeled around, and slammed the door behind her.

She leaned against it, clutching *The Lost One* to her ribs.

Now what?

She was still trapped in the dark with one long-dead girl, a ghost dog, and some silent, lurching thing in a long black cloak. Could a closed door keep any of them out anyway? Fiona couldn't even believe she was asking herself the question.

Quickly she scanned the room around her. Tall bookshelves, wood-paneled walls, one latticed window. There was no way out but the door behind her.

And now she could feel, seeping around the edges of that door, a sharpening edge of cold in the air.

Fiona pressed her back to the door as hard as she could.

A damp chill slithered around her ankles.

No, Fiona told herself. *The Searcher is a lie. The Searcher is a lie.*

She waited, shuddering, holding her breath.

Slowly, so slowly that it made her want to scream, the swirl of cold air faded away.

Fiona's knees gave out. She sank to the floorboards, spine still pressed to the door.

Fumbling through her backpack, she pulled out the flashlight and switched it on, slashing its frail beam around the room. Maybe she'd find something useful: a tool, a phone, a hidden exit.

Fiona steered the beam back to her lap, where it outlined the green leather edges of the book. Margaret had pushed *The Lost One* into her hands. There must have been a reason—something else in the book that she was meant to notice.

She flipped rapidly through the chapters to the end.

But the end wasn't where it had been before.

There were new pages. Waiting for her.

Heart thudding, hands shaking, Fiona began to read.

Stories are strange creatures.

Like the contents of a sealed and buried box, they exist only in the minds of those that recall them.

If a story isn't shared, if it isn't kept alive through the telling and retelling, it ceases to exist. If the last keeper of a tale dies without passing it along, the tale dies as well. And when a true story dies, perhaps the truth dies too.

This is a story of two sisters who did everything together.

But only one of them disappeared.

The other sealed and buried their story deep inside herself, where no one but her sister could have ever reached.

On the morning after the terrible thunderstorm, downed tree limbs, wide puddles, and shoals of wet leaves littered their small New England town. The sky was gray, the ground dark and damp. The river beneath Parson's Bridge swirled high around the pilings. The rush of its swollen waves could be heard deep in the heart of the Enchanted Forest, where Pearl was seated on a fallen log.

Of course, without her sister to play in it, the Enchanted Forest was just another part of the woods. But it was still a pretty spot, and a slightly drier one than the sunken stretches along the riverbanks. Pearl had brought her notebook and pencils with her. She was writing a fairy tale about two sisters and ignoring the dampness that seeped from the mossy tree trunk straight through her dress.

It was odd to be there without Hazel. The sisters hadn't spoken in nearly two days, not since they had argued at the carnival in the meadow and Pearl had run home alone. It was the longest they had ever gone without exchanging words. Oh, they had had other arguments, of course—dozens in a single day—but this was the first time that their anger had grown wide and deep enough to carve a chasm between them.

Pearl didn't know how the trouble would end. However, she knew Hazel, and she knew that their battle was far from over. In a way, she hoped it would continue. At least the battle was something they did together.

A rustle came from the ferns to Pearl's left.

Pearl paused her pencil, listening.

"Pixie?" she called out. "Is that you? Come here, boy!"

But Pixie did not appear. The ferns, and the woods around them, hushed. Only a few birds twittered in the treetops beneath the smoke-colored sky.

Pearl squinted back down at the open page. Maybe

when she was finished, she'd let Hazel read the story. Maybe then Hazel would understand.

Pearl caught herself. No. She was still angry at Hazel. Hazel didn't deserve her forgiveness.

. . . But perhaps Pearl would give it anyway. Because, although Pearl hated to admit it, life without her sister's company was proving to be drab and dull indeed.

She was bowing over the open pages once more when there came a louder, closer rustle.

A shadow poured across her notebook.

Pearl turned with a gasp.

A black hooded figure loomed above her.

Pearl shrieked as the Searcher raised a hand—an ordinary human hand—and smeared a fistful of mud across the open page.

"There!"

The other hand threw back the deep hood, revealing Hazel's laughing face. Pixie bounded out of the ferns beside her, dashing around the pair in happy, barking circles.

"*You?*" choked Pearl.

Hazel let out another peal of laughter. "You should *see* the look on your face!" She leaned against a tree, holding her sides. "Oh, Pearl! Your eyes are like goose eggs!"

Pearl jumped off the log, every thought of peace-making flying from her mind. "Why would you do that? Why do you have to be so hateful?"

"Because you deserved it," said Hazel, her laughter ceasing at last. "Now we're even. Or closer to even." She stepped toward Pearl. "This all started because you wouldn't listen to me and got us both into trouble."

"Into trouble?" Pearl echoed. "I was almost caught by the Searcher! And now you come here, dressed like that, to scare me?" She stood toe-to-toe with her sister, her fury flaring. "Hazel, I was nearly *taken*!"

Hazel broke into laughter once more. "Oh, you were not, you ninny. There is no Searcher."

Pearl could have kicked her. "Hazel, I *saw* it. I felt its hand on my neck."

"I know you did. But it wasn't the Searcher." Hazel spread her arms in their big sleeves. "It was just Matthew from the carnival, dressed in this old magician's cloak."

Pearl stepped backward. "What?"

"We thought it would be funny if he followed you and gave you a scare. So he pretended to be the Searcher. That's all." Hazel lowered her arms. "The Searcher is just a silly old story, and you're a silly little girl for believing it."

Pearl stared at Hazel, her thoughts spinning, her heart crumpling.

Then, before Hazel could brace for it, Pearl dropped her book and pencil, lowered her head like a charging bull, and barreled straight into her sister's stomach.

The two of them fell to the muddy ground.

Pearl was shorter and lighter, but she had surprise on her side, and at first she kept the upper position. Her advantage didn't last long, however. Once Hazel managed to brace a boot heel in the mud, she flipped Pearl onto her back, knocking the wind out of her. Hazel knelt above her, trying to catch her writhing arms.

"Get off me!" Pearl yowled.

"You started it!" Hazel shouted back. "Do you give in?"

In answer, Pearl shoved off from a nearby tree trunk, sending Hazel toppling over once more. The two of them rolled through bracken and mud, Pixie dancing around them, barking uproariously at the fun.

"You're not going to win, you little idiot!" Hazel yelled, pinning Pearl to the ground under her knees. "Tell me that you give in, or I'll give you another haircut!"

Pearl ceased struggling. She sagged back against the mud and leaves, panting. Hazel relaxed her grip, panting too. Seeing her chance, Pearl lunged forward and snatched the knife from Hazel's pocket, where it was always kept. As Hazel sat up, trying to grab it back, Pearl kicked her sister in the ribs, knocking her aside. Hazel let out a gasp of pain. But Pearl only scrambled upright and dashed off into the trees.

"Come back here!" Hazel shouted, once she could take a breath. "Give me back my knife!"

"I won't!" Pearl shouted back. "I'm going to throw it from Parson's Bridge!"

"You will not!"

"See if I don't!"

The sisters hurtled through the woods, darting between the thick trees, skidding in the mud. Hazel's stride was longer, but the cloak slowed her down, and she clutched her hurt ribs as she ran. Pixie galloped at her heels.

"Don't you dare throw my knife in the river, Pearl!" she shouted.

"You can't stop me!"

"If you even try it, I'll tell Mrs. Rawlins everything! I'll tell her you attacked me! That you kicked me while I was lying in the dirt!"

The truth in Hazel's words was almost enough to stop Pearl's heart. While Pearl and Hazel had found many ways to hurt each other, they had never before done physical harm. Now Pearl had changed everything. Hazel may have tricked her, but this terrible step forward was Pearl's own fault.

Pearl tried to sound uncaring. "Well, I'll tell her that you and Matthew were the ones who started it all by pretending to be the Searcher!"

"You won't get to tell her anything!" Hazel yelled. "Not when I get home first!"

Pearl glanced back at this.

Hazel had veered away from their usual track,

rushing downhill toward the riverbank. Pixie ran loy-
ally after her.

"Hazel, you can't take the shortcut!" Pearl yelled.
"Hazel!"

Hazel didn't reply.

Pearl hesitated.

If she ran on, she had a decent chance of reaching
the house before Hazel—but that would mean leaving
Hazel to cross the half-submerged tree, in the rushing
water, all alone.

Pearl turned back.

"Hazel!" she called, running down the bank. "You
can't cross there now! The water's too high!"

Hazel was already clambering onto the dead tree.
"Some people aren't afraid of every little thing," she
retorted. The muddy black cloak trailed around her.
Pixie, unwilling to follow any farther, skittered back
and forth on the bank beside the tree's dead roots,
whining.

"It's not because I'm afraid, it's because I'm not stupid!" Pearl shouted back. "Hazel! Hazel, stop!"

Hazel refused to cast her a glance. She walked out
onto the half-submerged trunk, one cloaked arm spread
for balance, the other still clutching the ribs where
Pearl's kick had landed. The water beneath her was
foamy, whirling, rushing.

Pearl turned away. "I'm going to take the bridge, and I'll still get home before you!"

She jogged off toward the bridge, taking a last glance over her shoulder to see whether Pixie had followed *her*, for once.

And Hazel was gone.

Pearl spun toward the shore. Perhaps Hazel had thought better of her plan and turned back. But Pixie was still there, beside the downed tree, facing the water. The dog gave another bark. And another, louder still.

Its desperation made Pearl's stomach twist.

"Hazel?" She hurried back along the muddy bank. The river was glutted with rainwater, sloshing so powerfully against each log and rock in its course that Pearl might easily have missed another splash. She ran down the slope into the water, letting it soak and ruin her leather shoes. Even one foot deep, she could feel its forceful pull. "Hazel!"

In the deeper water, far out of her reach, Pearl thought she glimpsed a flowing black shape. It was gone again in an instant.

Pearl shoved Hazel's stolen knife down the front of her underdress. Then she plunged into the water on the tree's upstream side. Both she and Hazel were strong swimmers, but they never swam in the river, even when the water was low and warm. Its current was too strong, its rocks sharp, its course deep. Now, in the swollen waves, Pearl barely managed to keep her head above water.

She dove beneath the surface, first reaching with both hands toward the spot where she had seen the dark shape, then reaching for anything at all. The water was icy cold. Soon her limbs would no longer do as she wished. Her numbed fingers wouldn't grasp; her lungs wouldn't hold air. Exhaustion seeped into her like the water itself.

Pearl knew the truth then. She had failed. She was too late to reach her sister. She was too late even to pull her own defeated body back to the bank. At least she and Hazel would be together, here, in the dark green quiet. And that seemed only right.

But somehow her body refused to sink.

Pearl rolled, groping through the waves. Her skirt had snagged on a jut of the fallen tree, keeping her from being swept under. She managed to clamber around the tree's side and break the surface for a breath. She struggled to free herself, popping two buttons and yanking the sodden linen dress straight over her head, leaving her in her underdress. With arms like wet ribbons, she grasped the tree. From there, she dragged herself, very slowly, to the riverbank.

For a while—Pearl had no idea how long—she sat on the muddy shore. Pixie stood motionless beside her.

It seemed to her that the sky began to darken. Perhaps afternoon had become evening. Perhaps the cold in the air was the approach of night. Or perhaps it was only the world around her realizing, as she had, that everything was now terribly, irreparably wrong.

When she finally rose to her bare feet and staggered through the woods toward Parson's Bridge, Pearl did not know she was doing it. When she crossed the lawn behind the grand brick house, when she was spied and caught and bundled inside by the help, Pearl didn't feel it. The story that she eventually told, of the Searcher stealing her sister away, didn't seem like a story at all. It seemed more true, more possible, than the thought that Hazel had drowned, and that it was Pearl's fault.

She hadn't seen or heard Hazel slip, after all. The dark thing in the water might have been anything or nothing. Hazel might have swum away, slipped off into the woods, and tricked her once more. She might be—she must be— somewhere out there, even now.

Because how could Hazel be gone, when Pearl was still alive? Who could look at Pearl and not see the shadow of the sister who should have been standing beside her?

The questions drifted through Pearl's whirling mind. When they settled at last, they had formed the start of a new story, one in which Hazel might still be found. One in which mystery and hope mixed together, and a dark-robed stranger would carry the blame.

The other version of the story would stay sealed inside her, buried like the pocketknife that Pearl would soon hide beneath the oak trees, known only by two people: Pearl, and her sister, who would never forgive her.

But who would also never tell.

Fiona flipped to the next page.

But this time, there wasn't one. She had reached the back cover. This was the end of the story.

Fiona sagged back against the door.

Evelyn Chisholm had drowned.

Her little sister, Margaret, was the only one who knew the truth—and, because she blamed herself, she had kept it hidden all this time.

Something strong and ugly writhed through Fiona's heart.

She didn't want to believe it. She didn't want Margaret to be at fault. Evelyn had brought the trouble on herself, hadn't she? Playing tricks, using the Searcher to terrify her younger sister. She had chosen to take that dangerous shortcut. Fiona pictured her crossing that slippery log, the river rushing beneath, one foot starting to slide . . . and suddenly the girl in her mind didn't look like Evelyn Chisholm at all. She had a sleek black ponytail and graceful posture, and when she plunged into the water, Fiona sucked in a breath so hard it made her own ribs ache.

Maybe . . .

Maybe what was haunting this place wasn't the Searcher, or an unfinished story. Maybe it was guilt.

Memories of an untied skate lace and a hidden medal and a trashed bedroom flickered through the back of Fiona's mind.

Maybe Margaret could still repair things somehow. Maybe if she faced the truth, that could be enough. Maybe she just needed someone—someone who truly understood—to help her move forward.

Shoving *The Lost One* into her backpack, Fiona wobbled to her feet. She peered through the creaking door into the darkness.

The second-floor walkway was empty. Fiona brushed the flashlight beam back and forth, making sure. No one else was in sight. The house's soft hums and groans were the only sounds. But patches of thick darkness were everywhere, around every corner, lurking in every doorway. Anything could be hiding in it, watching and waiting for her.

No, Fiona reminded herself. There was no Searcher. Whatever she had seen in the doorway was some mixture of Margaret's guilt and imagination and memory. Maybe a bit of Fiona's own guilt was tangled up in it too.

She just needed to find Margaret. And she couldn't let an old story, true or not, get in her way.

Fiona crept into the corridor.

Where would Margaret have gone? Fiona was hesitating, still trying to guess, when from somewhere below there came the whine of a dog.

Fiona hurried to the grand staircase. The portrait of Margaret Chisholm, with its frozen smile and strange eyes, watched her scurry down the steps.

She crept across the reading room. Every tiny sound and shifting shadow made her heart stutter. Another, louder whine cut through the dark, and Fiona almost squeaked with surprise—until she realized it had come from a floorboard under her own foot.

She slunk toward the circulation desk. There were no more sounds to follow now, but as she turned to the left, Fiona sensed something else—a faint, cool, swirling breeze. The kind of breeze that comes through an open door.

She followed it into the STAFF ONLY hallway.

Her flashlight gleamed over the wood-paneled walls. The office at the end of the hall was shut. But the door to the former kitchen stood wide open.

Fiona aimed her flashlight through the doorway. Its beam struck packed storage shelves, old counters, scuffed wooden floors. Another cold whirl of air swept past. And carried on it, from somewhere not too far away, was the sound of a sob.

Fiona scurried across the kitchen, winding through the shelves until she came face-to-face with a gaping black hole.

An open door.

A door to the basement.

Fiona could think of at least ten thousand things she would rather have done than wander around in the basement of this particular house.

But as she stood there, poking weakly at the darkness with her little flashlight, there came another sob. Clearer now. Closer.

Before any fears could stop her, Fiona flew down the creaking staircase.

The basement had the clammy coldness of wet laundry, or of mossy river stones. By the beam of her flashlight, Fiona could make out a cavernous, twisting chamber that bent around corners and through passageways. She spotted mounds of broken old furniture, piles of empty crates, crusty cans of paint. The rafters hung with cobwebs as thick as wool.

A stifled sob floated toward her.

"Margaret?" Fiona called. "Where are you?"

There was a moment of quiet.

Then, very softly, a voice answered.

"Here."

As soft as it was, the voice had an echo, as though the cold stone walls all around were answering too.

Fiona inched closer. Her flashlight cut a wavering path through the dark. And there, looming in the darkest corner, was a huge stone box.

A SARCOPHAGUS! shouted a voice in Fiona's mind.

But that was ridiculous. There wouldn't be an ancient burial vault in the basement of an old New England house. Besides, this box was even larger than a sarcophagus, with walls that were nearly eight feet high.

"Margaret?" Fiona whispered. "Are you in there?"

"I'm here," said the small, sad voice. "In the empty cistern."

Cistern. A big tank for storing water, Fiona remembered. That made more sense. "Why are you in there?"

"It seemed like the safest place," the voice whispered. "Evelyn always said that if we hid inside, no one would ever look for us in here. But I was always afraid to do it." There was a sniffle. "Now that doesn't matter."

"Margaret." Fiona stepped to the cistern's side. Its

stone was rough and damp, unpleasant against her palm. "I read the rest of your story. About how you and Evelyn fought. How she took the shortcut across the river and fell in. All of it."

There was another moment of quiet.

"Then you know it was all my fault," said Margaret's voice at last.

"But it wasn't," Fiona argued. "It was Evelyn's choice to cross where she knew it wasn't safe. What happened was just an accident."

"That wasn't all," Margaret's voice came back. There was a cold brittleness to it now, an icy layer covering its words. "I *lied*. I made up a story, and I told it over and over, so no one else ever knew the truth. No one even knew where she was."

"I understand why you did it." Fiona pressed closer to the cistern wall. "You wanted it to be true so badly, you almost made yourself believe it. It was barely a lie at all." She put one palm against the stone. "But you can admit the *real* truth now, Margaret. And maybe you can let the story—and the Searcher, and the guilt, and everything . . . maybe you can let it go."

"How?" asked the voice.

"I'm not totally sure," Fiona admitted, wishing that Charlie and his confident know-it-allness were here to help her make a plan. "Maybe if you just apologize, and then if you forgive *yourself* . . . maybe that would help. Maybe the Searcher will disappear for good. Maybe the curse, or whatever it is, will be over."

"I can't," said the voice, growing smaller still. "I'm afraid."

"You could try," Fiona urged. "I'll be right with you the whole time."

"You're not even with me *now*," said the small, sad voice.

Fiona twitched the flashlight across the basement again, homing in on a sturdy-looking wooden box. She dragged it to the cistern and climbed on top.

"Come on, Margaret." Setting her backpack against the cistern wall, Fiona hauled herself up on both arms, just managing to peep over its stone rim. "I'm right here." The flashlight pointed at one inner wall of the cistern, and Fiona couldn't lift her weight from her arm to move it. But by its reflected light, she could catch part of a dark shape huddled below her.

"I can't," the voice whispered. "You're just going to trick me too."

"I'm not. I promise." Fiona wriggled forward, using her feet and elbows to heave herself farther over the cistern's edge. "Margaret, I—"

But at that instant, the flashlight flew out of her hand. It clacked against the cistern's inner wall, its beam of light catching a figure in a long black cloak before dying away.

A cold grip took Fiona's hands. She smelled mud. Rot. River water.

And then the coldness pulled her in.

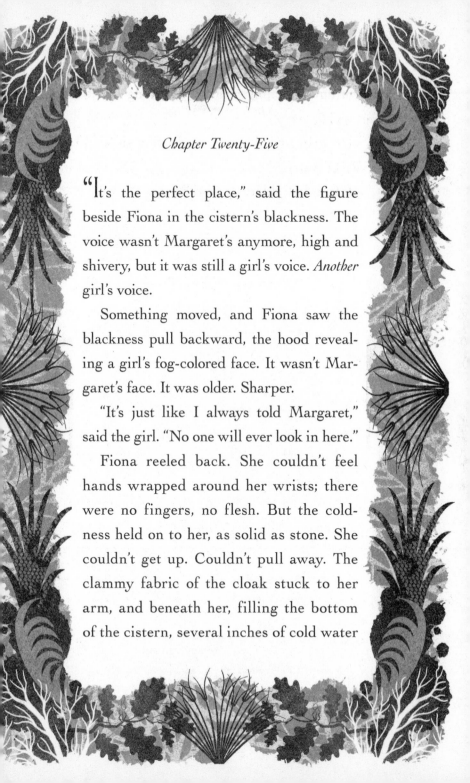

Chapter Twenty-Five

"It's the perfect place," said the figure beside Fiona in the cistern's blackness. The voice wasn't Margaret's anymore, high and shivery, but it was still a girl's voice. *Another* girl's voice.

Something moved, and Fiona saw the blackness pull backward, the hood revealing a girl's fog-colored face. It wasn't Margaret's face. It was older. Sharper.

"It's just like I always told Margaret," said the girl. "No one will ever look in here."

Fiona reeled back. She couldn't feel hands wrapped around her wrists; there were no fingers, no flesh. But the coldness held on to her, as solid as stone. She couldn't get up. Couldn't pull away. The clammy fabric of the cloak stuck to her arm, and beneath her, filling the bottom of the cistern, several inches of cold water seeped quickly through Fiona's clothes.

"*Evelyn,*" Fiona choked out. "I just—I just want to help."

The air grew icier as the other girl leaned close.

"This is how you help," she said. "You'll do what Margaret wouldn't. You'll stay."

Fiona wrenched her arm backward. She tried to wriggle to her feet, but the cold grip was unbreakable. At the same time, the water around her grew deeper. Chilly waves splashed against her legs.

"Even if I let go, you can't climb out," said Evelyn. "The walls are too high. That's why I tried to get Margaret to climb in with me. We could have helped each other out again. But she was a coward."

Fiona pawed at the cistern wall with her free hand, but Evelyn was right. There was nothing to climb. Nothing to hold on to.

"No one's going to find you," said Evelyn. Her voice wasn't cruel or taunting. It was merely calm. "No one will know where to look. Just like when they tried to find me."

Fiona thought of Charlie, dragged away by his grandmother. She thought of her parents, fast asleep in their bed. She thought of Arden.

Evelyn was right. No one was coming.

"Evelyn." Fiona squinted through the darkness, trying to meet the girl's eyes. "Please. *Please* let go."

The water rose higher. It seeped to the bottom of Fiona's ribs. The smell of the river—wet moss, dead leaves, rotting things—washed around her. And Evelyn held her down, as hard and heavy as an anchor.

"What happened to you wasn't fair," said Fiona desperately. "I know you're angry. You *should* be. But it wasn't anybody's fault."

"Not anybody's fault?" said Evelyn. "Margaret lied and lied and lied. She finally wrote the truth in a book that no one would ever read, and that no one would understand even if they *did* read it, and then she hid it in a room no one ever used. I had to move the book all around, hoping someone would finally find it. I had to put back the ending that Margaret erased, so that maybe, finally, someone would fit the pieces together and realize it was all true."

"You?" whispered Fiona. "You were the one who . . ." Panic squeezed her throat, and the words cut off. "So you were using it to—to lure me in?"

For a moment that felt like ages, Evelyn didn't answer.

"I don't like being alone," she said softly, at last.

"Margaret shouldn't have left you, Evelyn. She shouldn't have lied. But couldn't you just . . ." In the inky darkness, Fiona felt the water lapping against her neck. "Couldn't you forgive her?"

Evelyn ignored the question.

"It happens fast," she said instead. "You just go under. It doesn't hurt. And I'll be right here with you."

With a last, desperate burst, Fiona lunged sideways. She kicked both legs against the cistern wall, writhing, struggling to get her feet under her. But Evelyn's grip was like a clamp. Fiona couldn't stand up. All she managed to do was fill the cistern with waves, which crashed over her face. She spluttered, choking.

"Help!" she screamed, sucking in a wet breath. "Help! Somebody!"

"No one is coming," said Evelyn in a patient voice. "The ones who should find you will just let you go."

Fiona's mind flew to Arden once more. *I hope the Searcher finds you.*

Her sister hadn't just let her go. She had wished her gone.

The pain in Fiona's chest didn't just come from the lack of air anymore.

As the water closed over her, Fiona remembered sinking through the blue depths of that water-park pool, years ago. The pool that Arden had told her was safe.

No one was here to pull her out this time.

Evelyn was right. No one would find her. Not until it was too late.

Maybe not even then.

So the warm hands grabbing her didn't make sense.

She had to be hallucinating. Her air-starved brain was telling lies. But the hands kept pulling. Something—the sole of a shoe—kicked her in the side. The water was sloshing crazily, and light was coming from somewhere . . . not otherworldly, end-of-a-long-dark-tunnel light, but yellow electric light from a hanging bulb.

"Get up!" shouted Arden's voice. "Come on, Fiona!"

Fiona blinked. Through the water in her eyes, she could just make out her sister's face. Behind her, in the dark water, something else turned and thrashed, sending waves sloshing over the tank's side.

"Climb on my leg and I'll boost you over!" Arden commanded.

Fiona set a foot on Arden's knee, hauling her exhausted body onto the cistern wall.

"Now help me up!" shouted Arden.

Fiona squirmed around, her waist still balanced on the rim of the cistern, and reached down with her cold, wet hands.

Arden grabbed on. With a graceful jump, she swung one leg sideways, hooking a foot over the wall. Fiona's feet thumped to the floor. A second later, Arden's did too.

Near their soggy shoes, a curly brown dog paced frantically, eyes fixed on the top of the cistern. He let out a panicked whine.

"Hey," said Arden, crouching beside the spot where Fiona had dropped, gasping. "Are you okay? Can you breathe?"

Fiona nodded.

She stared past Arden, breathing hard, as something emerged from the cistern. A girl with fog-pale skin, a black cloak, and trailing dark hair clasped the cistern's side. A second later, another girl lunged up beside her, half hauling, half shoving the first girl over.

Pixie yipped.

"Go on, Evelyn!" Margaret's voice commanded. "Climb out!"

"You don't need to rescue me, you little idiot!" Evelyn jumped to the basement floor, long black cloak splaying like a puddle around her. Fiona and Arden scuttled backward.

"You're too late," said Evelyn. "*Much* too late."

Margaret, with her soaked dress and lank hair, slid down to the floor. "I know that, Evelyn." Her voice was smaller than her sister's, but clear enough to ring across the stony basement. "I know I'm too late. That doesn't mean . . . it doesn't mean I can't try."

Arden put one protective arm in front of Fiona.

"What's going on?" she whispered. "Who are these girls?"

"They used to live here," Fiona whispered back. "A long time ago."

Arden didn't ask anything else. But her body stiffened like a stretched string, ready to fly.

Evelyn, in her trailing black cloak, stared through the light at Margaret. Her hollow eyes were unreadable. Pixie quivered beside her, glancing desperately back and forth between his two girls.

"You climbed into the cistern," Evelyn said at last. "I thought you'd be too afraid. Like always."

"I *was* afraid," Margaret whispered. "But I did it."

"And you tried to swim in that part of the river," Evelyn added, after a long beat.

"Of course I did, Evelyn. I tried and tried. I wouldn't ever have stopped, but the branches—" She broke off, voice choking. "I *tried*."

Pixie nudged her hand with his nose.

"I didn't see you fall, Evelyn." Margaret's whisper was ragged now. "So I thought . . . or I wanted to think . . . that something else could have happened. That you had just . . . gone away." She paused, and Pixie nudged her hand again. "Because then maybe you would come back."

Evelyn didn't speak.

Margaret seemed to steel herself. She squared her

shoulders, her pale shape shifting under the gold electric light. "It wasn't a *lie*, Evelyn." She stepped toward her sister. "It wasn't. It was just the story I had to tell myself."

Evelyn didn't move. Pixie, Fiona, and Arden all kept silent, watching, waiting.

"The story didn't even change anything," Margaret went on. "Everyone blamed me anyway. And I blamed myself." She spread her hands. "For the rest of my life, I was—I was just your sister. I was the sister of that girl who disappeared."

"So you felt guilty," Evelyn said flatly. Softly. "You should have."

"But that isn't it." Margaret spread her hands. "Feeling guilty was nothing compared to how . . . how much . . ." Her voice broke into whispered fragments. "How much I *missed* you." She took a tiny step forward. "I missed you so much, Evelyn. I missed you all this time."

Evelyn kept still, letting her sister finish, her hollow eyes fixed hard on Margaret's face.

For a moment, everything was quiet. Fiona could feel the droplets of water trailing from her hair down the back of her neck. She could feel Arden breathing beside her.

At last Margaret reached into the pocket of her skirt. She pulled out the mother-of-pearl-handled knife.

Evelyn glanced at it. She let out a tiny sound, something closer to a laugh than anything else. "You want to give back what you stole from me?" The words were sharp. Their tone wasn't. "It's too late for that too."

Margaret waited, holding out the knife. "I know," she said.

When Evelyn still didn't take it, Margaret turned the knife around. She pulled the blade out of its handle. Then she grasped a hank of her long hair, pulled it tight, and sawed it off just above the roots.

Evelyn went perfectly still.

"You did this for me once." Margaret lowered her hand, the cut strands dangling from her ice-colored fingers. "Mrs. Rawlins was so angry. Remember?"

There was a long, silent breath.

"She said we looked like two half-plucked chickens," said Evelyn quietly.

"But you just laughed. We both laughed." Margaret sliced through another handful of hair. When she spread her fingers, the scattered strands disappeared before they touched the floor.

"Margaret." Evelyn gave a soft snort. "You look ridiculous."

One corner of Margaret's mouth curled upward. "Like a half-plucked chicken?"

Evelyn's mouth started to curl. Suddenly, like

someone pulling a cork from a bottle, she let out a laugh. *"Exactly* like a half-plucked chicken."

Margaret began to smile back. Pixie's tail wagged wildly.

Fiona glanced over at Arden, who was watching everything with wide eyes. Having her sister beside her in this impossible moment made the moment feel even more impossible. And at the same time, it made her feel something else—something like certainty. Because if Arden was here, Fiona belonged here too.

"Evelyn," said Margaret, her voice dwindling to a whisper again. "I'm so sorry."

"Oh, stop it." Evelyn placed a hand on Pixie, who was wriggling against her side. "You didn't make me take that shortcut. And you couldn't have stopped me, either."

"I should have tried harder. I should have told the whole truth. Not pretended that you could come back."

"I told you to stop, Margaret." Evelyn pulled the knife from Margaret's hand. "Besides, you were right. In a way." She folded the blade into its handle. "I *did* come back."

Then she slipped the knife into her own pocket, where it belonged.

Both pairs of sisters stepped through the library's back door. It must have been past midnight, Fiona realized.

The night was dark and far from over, but the clouds above the lawn had thinned, letting moonlight reach the woods below. The river glimmered through the trees.

Evelyn and Margaret led the way. They walked arm in arm, their old-fashioned shoes stepping in matching rhythm. Margaret's hair, suddenly long and smooth again, drifted in the breeze. Evelyn's long black cloak had disappeared, and her dress, pale linen like her sister's, billowed gently behind her. Pixie bounded beside them.

Fiona and Arden followed, side by side.

"Hey, Arden?" Fiona asked softly, as they climbed down toward the bank. "How did you know?"

Arden's eyes flicked toward her. "How did I know to come and get you? I didn't." She shrugged. "After you left, I just couldn't sleep. I sat by the windows in my room, waiting for you to come home. Finally it had been so long, I started to think—" She halted. "I thought maybe what I'd said had come true. So I grabbed my bike and rode to the library."

"You could have just told Mom and Dad," said Fiona, climbing over a fallen tree. "You didn't have to come out by yourself in the middle of the night."

"That would have taken more time, waking them and explaining everything. And you would have gotten into huge trouble. And I just . . ." Arden paused again. "I had to make sure you were okay. Myself."

They reached the riverbank. For a moment, the muddy smell of the water made Fiona's steps falter. The waves closing over her face in the old cistern had smelled just the same. But here, there was moonlight and wind and the scent of fresh leaves. And Arden was beside her.

Margaret and Evelyn started across Parson's Bridge, Pixie pattering ahead. Their feet made only the softest sounds on the wooden boards.

Fiona and Arden tagged after. The two of them were walking fast, but somehow they were falling farther behind.

"When you got to the library," Fiona asked, "how did you find me? How did you know where to look?"

Arden's profile was silvery in the moonlight. "When I got there, the front doors were wide open. I ran inside, but everything was dark, and while I was trying to find the lights, that dog came running up to me, barking its head off. And then I saw that girl, running down a hallway. . . ." She pointed toward Margaret, ahead of them. "I followed her to the basement. Even though you know I *hate* basements. And even though I could tell she wasn't . . . she wasn't really . . ."

Fiona met her sister's eyes. "They've both been gone for a long time."

"Well, at least . . ." Arden broke off with a little shudder in her voice. "At least they found each other again."

Fiona looked down. Arden's steps were shaky too. She hadn't noticed it before, with the darkness and uneven ground, but Arden was limping.

"Hey," she said. "Are you hurt?"

"No. Not really." Arden shook her head. "I just landed wrong on one ankle when I jumped out of that water tank. I'm fine."

"Are you sure?"

Arden hesitated for a split second. "I don't know. But that's okay. You're here, and I'm here, and we're okay."

"If you need to lean on me or anything," said Fiona, "you can."

"Thanks," said Arden. "If I need to."

They had reached the denser woods on the far side of the bridge. The Chisholm sisters were many steps ahead of them now, their dresses just pale spots between the thick trees.

"Where are we going, anyway?" Arden asked.

"To the Enchanted Forest, I think. It's part of the woods where the sisters used to go. They named all the trees and decorated them and made up stories and stuff. It was their special place."

"Hey, Fifi," said Arden. "Do you remember the Hidden Cavern?"

Fiona *hadn't* remembered. But Arden's words brought it back: the low, crooked nook underneath the staircase at Grandma Crane's house, where she and Arden had played during every summer visit.

"The Hidden Cavern," Fiona breathed. "I haven't thought about that in forever."

"Well, you were only five when Grandma moved out of that house," said Arden. "I wanted to imagine that it was a secret room full of jewels in an old castle, but you wanted to say it was a hole full of dinosaur bones."

"So we pretended it had both." Fiona smiled. "Jewels and dinosaur bones."

The ground sloped beneath them, guiding them down into a patch of ferns. The surrounding trees, tall as church steeples, whispered softly. Fiona gazed around. Even in the middle of the night, this grove looked green. It smelled and *felt* green too, full of things that would always be alive and growing, even when they were hard to see.

"Where did they go?" Arden asked.

Fiona pulled her eyes back to the ground.

The sisters had vanished.

She scanned the trees in every direction, but there were no summery linen dresses, no heads of long brown hair. She thought she heard a single bark from Pixie, somewhere very far away. But that was all.

She and Arden were alone in the leafy moonlight.

Once there were two sisters who did everything together, Fiona thought.

They stood still for a long, quiet minute, breathing in the silvery air.

"We should get home," Arden said at last. "I really hope Mom and Dad didn't get up for a midnight snack or anything."

"Yeah." Fiona turned away from the grove. Her stomach, no longer twisted up with fear, gave a low growl. "Now *I* really want a midnight snack."

"You know what we should do?" said Arden as they headed toward Parson's Bridge. "Make ice-cream sundaes. If Mom and Dad wake up, we can say that's what we were doing all along."

"Yes!" Fiona smiled. "Let's run and get our bikes!"

Arden's face shifted. "I don't know if—" She broke off. "I'm not sure I should try to run on this ankle. I mean, it's probably fine. I just . . . never mind. You should go ahead. You'll get home faster."

"No," said Fiona quickly. "I'll walk with you. And you should hold my arm, just in case."

"Okay. Fine." Arden took Fiona's elbow. "We can call this the favor you owe me."

"What? No way." Fiona turned to watch her sister's face. "The favor should be something big."

Arden didn't look down, but she held Fiona's arm a little closer. "Like you coming to watch me skate sometime?"

"No," said Fiona again. "That's not a favor. That's just something I should do."

There was a beat.

"Okay," said Arden. And Fiona could see her smile, even through the darkness. "We'll save it for another time, then."

And they stepped onto the old wooden bridge together.

Chapter Twenty-Six

Three days later, when Charlie was finally allowed to leave his house, Fiona told him the whole story over cinnamon buns at the Perch Diner.

It took a long time, because he kept interrupting, and they had to go silent whenever Judy or other diners came near their booth, and by the time Fiona reached the end of the tale, over an hour had passed.

It was funny, Fiona thought, how short hours became when you were with certain people. Time had always flown when she was with Cy and Nick and Bina. Sitting here with Charlie felt almost like being with one of them—except instead of feeling comfortable and familiar, this felt new and *un*familiar. And that was good too.

"There's one more thing," said Fiona. "When I got home that night, *The Lost One* had already disappeared from my backpack. I thought it might have gone back to the library again. But when I sneaked up to the third floor to check Evelyn's room, it wasn't there either. It wasn't anywhere."

"That makes sense," said Charlie, looking annoyingly unsurprised. "The book doesn't need to be read anymore. It's done."

"I guess so," said Fiona. She felt heavy and empty at the same time. A lot like a blank leather-bound book.

Charlie cut a bite of cinnamon bun but didn't eat it. "I wish I had been there," he said, looking down at the tabletop.

"Me too," Fiona answered.

Although she only said it to be kind.

If Charlie had stayed at the library with her, everything would have been different. Arden wouldn't have had to jump into the cistern and haul Fiona out. The two of them wouldn't have walked through the moonlit woods, ridden their bikes across the sleeping town, or sat on the kitchen floor eating giant bowls of ice cream at two thirty in the morning. Fiona wouldn't know, not for certain, how many rules Arden would bend or how many chances she would take, just for her.

And Fiona liked knowing.

"It's weird," she said, turning her cocoa mug in circles. "I'm glad we know what really happened. I'm glad we helped. But I'm also kind of sorry that the story is done."

Charlie nodded. "I know what you mean. But stories are supposed to have endings. Plus, they can only *really* end if no one knows them. And you and I will remember this one."

"Yes." Fiona gave him a full smile now. "Definitely."

"So," said Charlie as Fiona scraped up a trail of icing. "You're still going to be here in the fall, right?"

"I'd say the odds are ninety-nine-point-five percent. Why?"

He shrugged, looking almost sheepish. "I was just wondering if you'll be going to school here. If you do, we'll be in the same grade."

"Oh." Fiona had barely thought about the school year. With all of summer stretching out ahead—a summer that had seemed so blank and lonely just a week ago—the next grade was a barely visible bump on the horizon. "Yeah. I suppose we will be."

"Good." Charlie flashed a smile. "It'll be great to have someone else around who . . . I mean, most of the kids here don't understand why someone would spend half their summer in a library."

Fiona scooped up the last drip of icing. "I don't understand why anyone *wouldn't*."

"Me neither," Charlie agreed. "When you get your

school schedule, you should show me. I know all the teachers, so I can tell you what they're like. And I can help you find your way around the school. It's not too big, but I still know all the best routes. And there's a science club. We invent things and solve problems and go to competitions. You could join us. If you want to."

Fiona grinned back. "That sounds great." She glanced at the clock above the pie display. "Ooh. I have to get home. I'm going to my sister's skating practice today." She slid her backpack over her arm. "Her ankle was sore, so she had to skip a couple of days, but she's feeling pretty much back to normal now."

"Hey," said Charlie again, as Fiona scooted toward the end of the bench. "Could I come with you and watch sometime? Like when there's a competition?"

Fiona halted. "You want to watch my sister skate?"

"I've never been to a figure-skating event," said Charlie simply. "I think it would be interesting. I like learning about new things."

"Yeah," said Fiona. Because Charlie was right. Arden was worth watching. "Sure. I'll let you know."

"Heading out?" asked Judy, marching up to the booth. "Nope. It's on the house," she added, as Fiona reached for her pocket. "Just bring your family in for pie some afternoon."

"That's what everyone around here does," Charlie added.

"I will." Fiona waved to them both. "Thank you. Bye!"

She hurried out into the late morning sun.

The town of Lost Lake was quiet, as usual. But something about that quiet had changed. It felt restful now, not watchful. Birds called to one another in the rustling oaks. Sunlight flickered against the shade. Through the trees, here and there, were silver-green glints of the river and lake, bright with sunlight on the surface, cradling old secrets in the dimness beneath. Fiona pedaled over the shady pavement, past the brick houses and white clapboard churches, down streets whose names belonged to Pearl and Hazel's story, and to her own.

Just one more turn, and she'd be home.

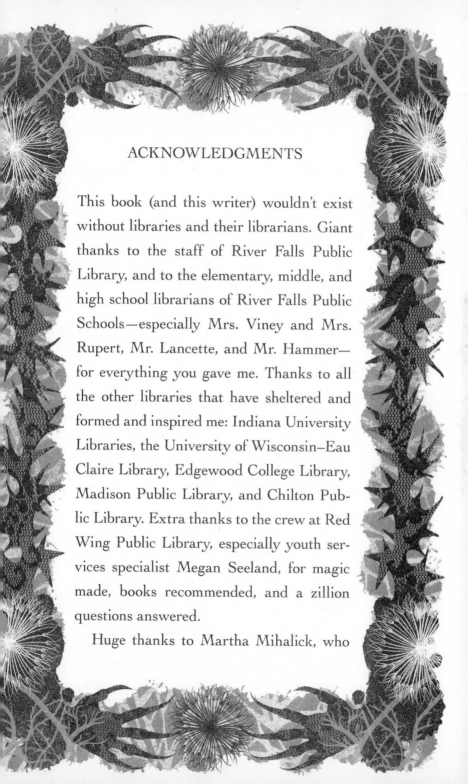

ACKNOWLEDGMENTS

This book (and this writer) wouldn't exist without libraries and their librarians. Giant thanks to the staff of River Falls Public Library, and to the elementary, middle, and high school librarians of River Falls Public Schools—especially Mrs. Viney and Mrs. Rupert, Mr. Lancette, and Mr. Hammer—for everything you gave me. Thanks to all the other libraries that have sheltered and formed and inspired me: Indiana University Libraries, the University of Wisconsin–Eau Claire Library, Edgewood College Library, Madison Public Library, and Chilton Public Library. Extra thanks to the crew at Red Wing Public Library, especially youth services specialist Megan Seeland, for magic made, books recommended, and a zillion questions answered.

Huge thanks to Martha Mihalick, who

finds me whenever I get lost, and to the whole Greenwillow family: Laaren Brown, Lois Adams, Virginia Duncan, Paul Zakris, Audrey Diestelkamp, Robby Imfeld, and Sam Benson. Thank you, thank you, thank you.

I don't know where I'd be without Danielle Chiotti. Thank you forever, Danielle. Endless thanks to Michael Stearns and everyone at Upstart Crow Literary, too.

The first time I saw the Balbusso twins' cover art, it took my breath away—and it still does, hundreds of times later. I could not be luckier. Grazie infinite, Anna and Elena.

Big thanks and love to my critique group—Anne Greenwood Brown, Connie Kingrey Anderson, Lauren Peck, Kristin Johnson, and Jennifer Kaul—for being there through pregnancies and pandemics and uncountable drafts. You're all gems.

Thanks to the Spooky Middle Grade and Minnesota kid lit communities, to the teachers and booksellers and book bloggers, and to the readers who are the reason for everything.

Finally, thanks and much love to my family: Mom and Dad, Dan, Katy, and Alex, and all the uncles and aunts (especially my favorite pediatric NP, Aunt Kris) and in-laws and cousins. And Ryan, Beren, and Vivien: If I've got you, I've got everything I need.